JOE'S CALLING

A MORGAN'S FIRE NOVEL

M. LEE PRESCOTT

Joe's Calling

By

M. Lee Prescott

Published by Mt. Hope Press
Copyright 2022, M. Lee Prescott
Cover Design: Ashley Lopez
Image credits: *stock.adobe.com/167198043* and *stock.adobe.com/487597261*

ISBN: 978-1-7379034-8-2 (print)

This book is a work of fiction. Names, characters, places, and events are products of the author's imagination or are used fictitiously. Any resemblance to actual people (alive or deceased), locales, or events is entirely coincidental.

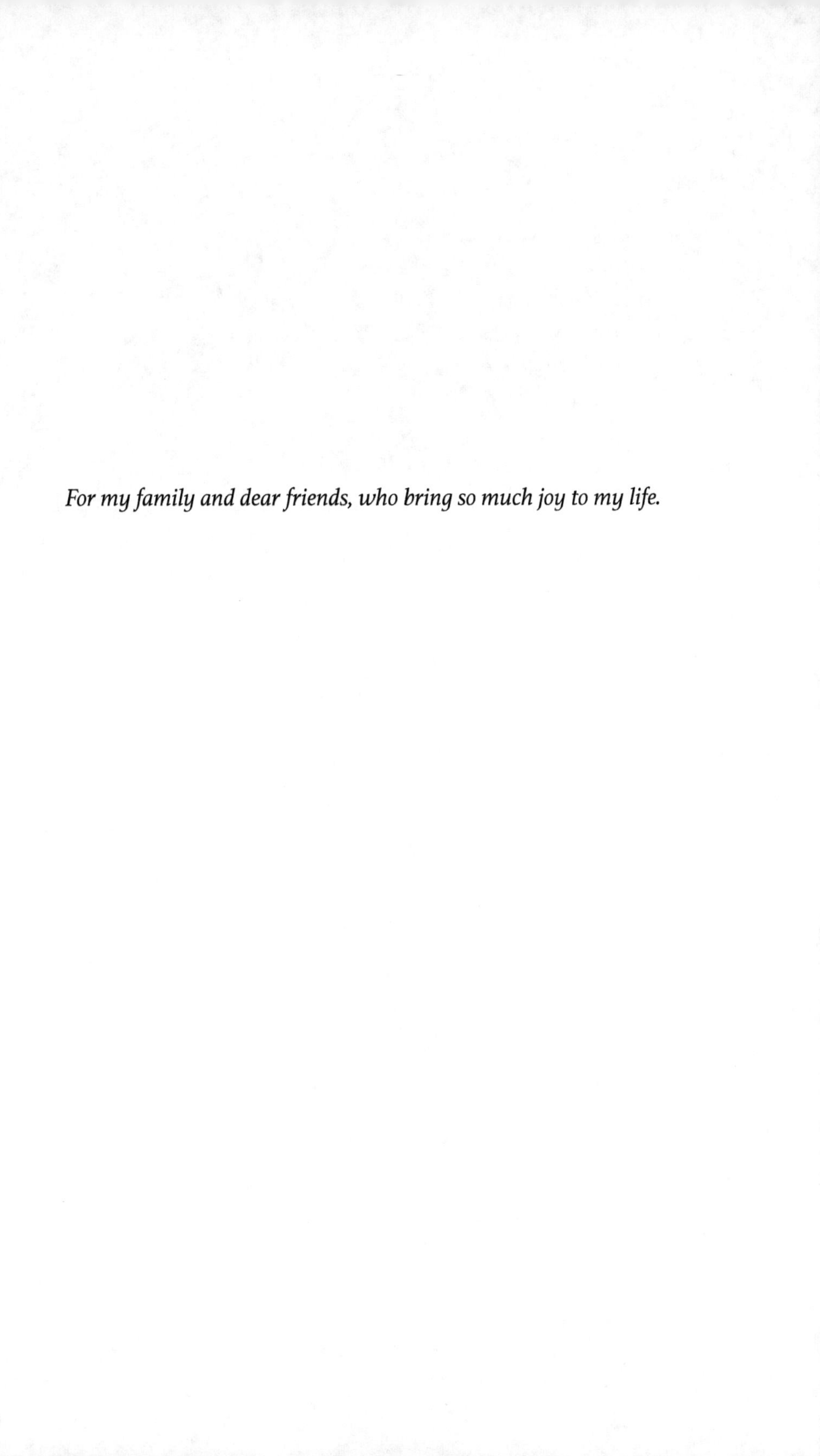

For my family and dear friends, who bring so much joy to my life.

CHAPTER 1

Afternoon light streamed into the space Joe O'Leary, ex-priest, social worker, and therapist, now called his office. He heard muffled footsteps above him, but otherwise, the old Victorian was silent. Peaceful. His last client had departed five minutes earlier and left the door ajar. Gazing out at the tangled garden behind the house, Joe leaned back, enjoying a last cup of Earl Grey before heading home. As he sipped the hot tea, he breathed in the scent of bergamot, fragrant, familiar, comforting.

A door opened in the hallway, and seconds later, his landlord, Andy Roby, popped his head in. "Hey, Joe, how're you settling in?" the accountant asked, his green eyes warm, sandy hair ruffled as if he'd been trying to pull it out. Short and a little pudgy, Andy had recently asked Joe if he'd like to be his running buddy. Ten years his senior, Joe was tall and lean. While his running days were mostly behind him, he had agreed, but they had yet to begin their exercise regimen.

"Great, thanks, Andy. I have about twenty regular clients and a few more about to begin."

The other man whistled, leaning his shoulder against the doorframe, scanning the room. "Wow, so quick? Have you been advertising?"

Joe smiled. "No, most of them are former parishioners. We have a different kind of relationship than before, but there's a sense of security, I suspect, in knowing your therapist. I've asked that they clear it with the new priest, Father Flynn. I did as well, as I don't want to step on his toes. Care for a cup of tea?"

"Thanks, but I've gotta run. Blind date. My sister's fixing me up. I'm pretty certain it will be a disaster, just like all the others."

"You never know," Joe said. Andy, forty years old, was divorced with two teenage children.

"That's the trouble. I know my sister. The women she thinks will be perfect for me never are. It's become my Friday night torture. Have a great weekend."

"You too."

"And let's set a start date for our morning jog. Maybe next Monday? You game?"

"I might be able to manage a lope."

"That should work since you're at least a foot taller, so you have a longer stride. You can lope and I'll scramble to keep up. Night."

"Night," Joe said, amused by the image Andy conjured up.

For many years, his Friday night routine involved picking up some kind of seafood takeout. Tonight, he decided to order a lobster roll from Bluewater Seafood, a popular restaurant near his house. He made the call, then leaned back in his chair to enjoy the remnants of his tea.

Invariably, in quiet moments, his thoughts drifted to Meryl Stockdale, chef at Field and Fire, the village's newest restaurant. *Meryl and her luminous blue eyes.* Months earlier, their lives had intersected over the holidays. There had been a spark, but it was too soon for him. Thus, by tacit agreement, they had gone their separate ways. *Is it time now?* He set his empty mug aside. He had strong feelings for her, of that he was certain. Whenever their paths crossed, his heart raced and his body temperature went through the roof. His feelings went beyond the physical, however. With Meryl, he glimpsed a home, a loving, nurturing home. Nowhere else, with no one else, did he experience peace and steadiness and the promise of a loving future.

~

FRIDAY NIGHT WAS HOPPING AT FIELD AND FIRE, THE FARM-TO-TABLE restaurant located on the vast Morgan's Fire property just north of the village of Horseshoe Crab Cove. Meryl tucked errant strands of sandy hair under her chef's hat as she surveyed the staff going about their work. She'd trained them well. She barely had time to appreciate how smoothly the kitchen was running before she got bumped from behind.

"Oh, Meryl! I mean Chef Stockdale, I am so sorry!" Lyddie Faulkner, one of their best waitresses, swung a full tray of entrées to the side, managing to avoid dropping them. In crisp white shirt and tailored black slacks, her blonde hair in a tight ponytail, she looked lovely as always, her pale cheeks now crimson.

Meryl smiled at the nineteen-year-old. "Good save. And you know it's Meryl, even when you're trying to run me down."

"I am so, so sorry. Are you okay?"

"More than okay. Now scoot or the food'll be cold."

As Lyddie disappeared, Rori Lake, the restaurant's comanager and Meryl's head chef, stepped into the kitchen. "What happened to the kid? She looks like a scared rabbit."

"We had a collision."

Rori flipped her long auburn hair to the side as she stared at the dining room door. "Doesn't sound like her. She's usually so cool, calm, and collected."

"Trouble in paradise, maybe?" Freddy Santos, the sous chef, remarked, as he added a handful of herbs to a platter of sautéed calamari. Meryl seldom put breaded and fried seafood on the menu, and the calamari was no exception. Lightly sautéed in olive oil, garlic, and a local farm's freshly picked sweet peppers, the dish was already a favorite of local diners and reviewers.

Rori turned to Freddy. "I'm sure there's a story there, but I can't stay to hear it. Later. Have either of you seen Murph?"

Her companions shook their heads. As she disappeared, Meryl

looked over at her sous chef. "You really shouldn't give her any ammunition, you know."

"I know, I know," Freddy said, sliding the platter of calamari aside, ready to be picked up. "It was just fresh in my mind since she and her hot boyfriend were squabbling in the back hall a few minutes ago."

"You don't miss much, do you, nosey?"

Meryl eyed her dark-haired chef, his smooth skin a deep copper against his tall, white hat. Freddy missed little with those coal-black eyes and razor-sharp hearing. It was unnerving. Wolfie Morgan, the hunky boyfriend to whom he referred, managed the Morgan's Fire winery. His father, Richard, owner of Morgan's Fire, was an investor in the restaurant.

"It's a gift. Hey, while we're gossiping, I haven't seen the ex-priest around lately. Are you keeping him under wraps?"

Now Meryl blushed. "No comment."

"Wonder if we'll be needing an extra bartender anytime soon." Joe sometimes tended bar when the restaurant had private functions.

"Not funny. Besides, Joe and I are just friends."

"Uh-huh. I certainly don't look at my friends the way you two goo-goo eye each other."

"Back to work!" she said, heading down to supervise at the other end of the room.

CHAPTER 2

Shortly after eleven, Meryl drove home, thinking back over the last six months and her previous life before landing in Horseshoe Crab Cove. Her much-older brother, Johnny, had suggested her for the Field and Fire job. He spent his summers cooking at Emma's Dream, a camp for handicapped children at the Morgan's Run Ranch in Arizona, home to Richard Morgan's brother, Ben. Semi-retired, Johnny only took "love jobs" nowadays. When Richard called asking for chef recommendations, he mentioned his "very talented sister."

Brother and sister had run several successful restaurants together on the West Coast, but only Johnny rose to the rare distinction of a fifteen star Michelin chef. When he retired from full-time work at their last restaurant, Meryl decided to take a break. She packed up and headed for Italy, where she spent several years living and working. She loved Tuscany, but finally knew it was time to come home. Her feet had barely touched the ground when Johnny called about the Field and Fire position. Owner Sandy Rodriguez flew her in from Chicago, where she was staying with Johnny.

One conversation with Sandy and Richard Morgan and a tour of the village did the trick. Meryl knew she'd found a home. Sandy was a great boss, she loved her coworkers and she'd happily settled into a rental house on the river. Life was good. Then Joe O'Leary came along. Their mutual attraction was obvious to anyone who saw them together, and Meryl was smitten from day one. Joe was handsome and kind, with a strength and depth to him she'd never seen in any other man. Eight years her senior, he radiated calmness and steadiness. In his presence, she experienced a sense of peace as well as an intense, surprising attraction.

Drawn as she was to him, she also knew that he had just stepped away from decades as a priest. Unsure what this transition meant, she intuited his need for time. She also believed that he should make the first move. Thus, she hung back, waiting. This was not the case with every single woman in the village, including Rori. Besieged by invitations and covered casseroles from the day he retired from the church, Joe had that to contend with as well.

As she pulled into her driveway, her cell rang. She fished the phone out of her bag and saw her brother's name. "Hello?"

"Hey, sis, how's tricks?"

"Great. Fine."

"You're not still slaving in the kitchen, are you?"

"Nope, just got home," she said, slipping out of her blue Mini Cooper and heading for her door. She sighed, the gentle sounds of the river lapping against the back porch greeting her.

"Let me unlock my door and then I'm all yours." She stepped into the cottage and set down her bag. She then slipped out of her shoes, poured a glass of seltzer, and padded out to the porch, where she settled on the worn but comfortable chaise.

"Okay, I'm ready. What's up?"

"Can't a brother call just to say hi?"

She chuckled, taking a sip of her drink. "Some can, not mine."

"Well, I'm calling on Sherry's behalf." Sherry was their half sister, born to their father after their parents' divorce. Sherry was ten years younger than Meryl. Their mother had died of breast cancer soon after the divorce, and Jim Stockdale, age fifty-eight, had married eighteen-year-old Sherry, a waitress in the local diner. The couple had rapidly produced two kids. When the youngest was barely out of diapers, Jim had died of a massive heart attack.

"Oh?"

"She lives not far from you now. Did you know that?"

Meryl ran her fingers through her hair, frowning. "No, but as you are well aware, Sherry and I aren't close."

"I know, hon. I'm not exactly calling for Sherry. It's about Gigi and Kip."

Meryl gritted her teeth. The last time she'd seen their niece and nephew, they'd been toddlers. Unruly, spoiled toddlers. "How are the little hellions?"

"Apparently, they're doing great. Their mom's dating a sailor. Well, tactician, really. He goes all over the world."

"Good for her."

"The boyfriend has an opportunity to deliver a big yacht to Valencia."

"Where's that, Florida?"

"Valencia, Spain. Sherry's all excited 'cause she's been invited to go with him, but she can't find anyone to watch the kids."

Meryl felt a headache creeping across her forehead. "No."

"Listen, sis. Before you say no. They're twelve and thirteen, not babies."

"Even worse. No."

"They'll only be gone for about three weeks. She says you can feel free to give the kids lots of jobs around the house or at the restaurant."

Like that's gonna happen, Meryl thought as she took a deep breath. "Have you forgotten that I work really long hours? I'm at the restaurant five, sometimes six days a week from morning till now."

"Look at your staff. That billionaire boss of yours let you hire nine underchefs. When did you and I have a staff of nine?"

"We didn't need them. We had each other."

"My point is you can take a few days off."

"If I had a few days, I'd find a beach in the tropics and do nothing."

"No, you wouldn't. You hate being idle. Come on. It might even be fun."

"I'll think about it."

"Sherry needs to know by tomorrow. They leave in three days."

"What are they going to do if I don't take them? Lock them in the house with a full refrigerator for three weeks?"

"Probably."

"Oh, for goodness' sake. Let me sleep on it. I'll let you know in the morning."

CHAPTER 3

Grouchy from lack of sleep and Johnny's call, Meryl rose at six and texted Johnny: *Bring them on.* She'd told her staff not to expect her till early afternoon, so she decided to walk into the village for coffee and a muffin. She slung her bag over her shoulder and grabbed a floppy hat for the half-mile stroll to the Crab Café along Beach Road to Main Street. As she stepped out the front door, she waved to Frankie Brown, her neighbor, out sweeping her front steps. Tall, with ramrod-straight posture and curly salt-and-pepper hair, the sixty-something Frankie lived in a house that belonged in Middle Earth. When she drove into her driveway, Meryl often expected to spy a hobbit peeking from the arched, oaken door.

"Can I bring you something from the Café?" she called.

"Thanks, but the Yarners will be here in half an hour."

Frankie was a member of the Darn Yarners, a group of village women who had been friends for over forty years. All in their sixties now, the group of eight civic-minded seniors were beloved by all in the village. Every one of the Yarners was still working. Frankie did a variety of jobs from painting and leaded glass construction to private investigating.

"Enjoy!" Meryl said as she turned toward the village. She envied the Yarners, who dined at Field and Fire at least once or twice a month and had shared so many of life's joys, sorrows, struggles, and celebrations. Like benevolent aunts, they were always there, lending support to one another and their extended families.

A breeze followed Meryl as she made her way to the village center. Several teenagers rode by on their bikes, headed for jobs in the village. The milk truck passed, and Mickey gave her a thumbs-up. They knew each other well as he delivered to the restaurant every day.

How did I get so lucky? she mused as Main Street came into view.

The Café was quiet, with only a few diners. She ordered a large coffee and a blueberry muffin, then took her breakfast to Laura's Community Garden, a short walk down Main Street. A favorite spot for villagers to picnic, enjoy their morning coffee, or relax in the shade, the communal space had been created by Pam Morgan, her boss's wife, in memory of her mother. The garden had recently been expanded to double the number of plots, but still there was a waiting list for garden space. Most gardeners had home gardens, but meeting friends and working together was a very different experience.

As Meryl walked through the gate, a half dozen people worked their plots, weeding and preparing the beds for planting over the next few weeks. She nodded or waved as she passed, headed for her favorite bench at the far end of the garden. Distracted by all her greetings and conversation, she hadn't looked ahead. If she had, she'd have seen that her bench was occupied.

"Great minds think alike," he said, rising to say good morning. He towered over her as they exchanged a friendly embrace.

"Joe... Hello, good morning," she sputtered, loving the warm twinkle in his dark brown eyes. Dressed casually in khakis and a blue shirt, he looked gorgeous. Although thin and lanky, he gave the best hugs, the kind that made one feel completely hugged. His former parishioners had been fortunate indeed. Absently, she wondered if Father Flynn gave great hugs too.

"Care to join me?"

Meryl sat down, careful not to spill her coffee. "Thanks. This is my favorite spot."

He looked over at her, smiling. "Mine too."

"Haven't seen you around lately," she said, gingerly opening her bag and extracting the warm muffin.

"Been busy setting up my practice and settling into village life. There's also the work involved in transitioning to a secular life."

Surprised, Meryl met his eyes. "Have you left the church completely, then?"

He chuckled. "No, I still attend mass in Southport. Holy Name."

"Not your old church?"

He shook his head. "No, I love St. Mary's by-the-Sea, but I wanted to give Father Flynn, my replacement, his space."

"That's kind of you."

He smiled. "A bit of self-preservation as well. Not sure how I'd feel with someone else in the pulpit. This way, I can give myself to God and the service with no past associations. The members of Holy Name have been very welcoming."

"I'm glad."

"So how about you? How are you doing? I hear raves about the restaurant from everyone. What's it been now?"

"Six months. It's been intense, but like everything Sandy Rodriguez touches, it's a grand success. I feel very lucky."

"I'm sure a large share of that success is yours. Are you enjoying village life and your home on the river?"

She nodded, taking a bite of muffin, then sipping her coffee. "It's a wonderful place. I have great neighbors, and everyone has been so friendly."

"So, all's well, then?" He stared at her, a question reflected in his eyes.

"I look a bit harried, don't I?"

Joe laughed. "No, just not as relaxed as the last time I saw you."

How is he so perceptive, she wondered. *Of course, he's spent a lifetime engaged in deep listening.* "My brother called last night on behalf of our half sister. She wants to send her two teenagers to stay with me for three weeks."

"Sounds like fun."

"Not when I work the hours I do. Besides, I barely know them. Sherry, my half sister, and I aren't close."

"You could always say no," he said as he crumpled the bag that had held his bagel and tossed it in a nearby trash can.

"They have no one else."

"So, you're leaning toward yes, then?"

Meryl shrugged, giving him a wan smile. "I guess I am."

"When do they arrive?"

"Tomorrow."

They chatted for almost an hour, sharing work stories and how they'd been spending their days. Finally, Joe stood. "I'd like nothing better than to stay here all day, but I have a client coming in a few minutes."

Meryl smiled, crumpling her empty muffin bag. "No worries. I should get back and prepare my guest quarters. It's wonderful to see you, Joe."

"You too." He stood, gazing down at her, his eyes thoughtful. "I wonder if... I mean to say, would you like to have dinner with me sometime?"

Meryl rose, looking up at him. "I'm usually busy at dinnertime, and I fear after tomorrow, I'll be busy keeping track of my guests."

"Of course. I wasn't thinking."

"Let's not give up. I've got an idea. Once the prep's completed and the dinner shift is going full tilt, I could delegate. As head chef, Rori can hold down the fort for a few hours. Would you be free around seven thirty tonight?"

"I would."

"How about eating in the winery's tasting room? It's lovely and always closed at night. I'm sure Wolfie won't mind. Sandy and Pam grab a meal over there once in a while when he's really busy."

"I'd love it. What can I bring?"

"Yourself. It's my treat. I'll pack a picnic basket, and we'll choose a wine and settle up with Wolfie tomorrow."

"Sounds perfect."

"Assume it's a go unless you hear from me by three. Shall we meet there at seven thirty, then?"

"I'll look forward to it."

They'd reached the garden gate, and she turned to him. "Well, I'll say goodbye."

"See you tonight," he said,

She reached out and touched his arm. "Yes, tonight. I'll make something nice."

CHAPTER 4

Shortly after noon, Joe closed his office door and headed down Main Street to have lunch with Murph O'Neill and Greta Jeffers at the Café. Murph was his landlord, an old family friend and former parishioner, but the reason for their meeting was to finalize plans for Murph and Greta's wedding. Joe had agreed to officiate informally. The ceremony was to be held at Greta's place of worship, the Quaker Meeting House. The small clapboard-sided meetinghouse was in Southport. Greta's parents, along with a handful of others, had started the Meeting shortly after moving to the area, and the tiny church continued to have a small but committed congregation. The couple had obtained the blessing of the Meeting to have a former Catholic priest perform the ceremony.

As he walked, he reflected on the morning and Meryl Stockdale's blue eyes, the color of the sky on a perfect day. He'd been stunned at the feelings she stirred in him. His body ached with a longing that both amazed and terrified him. *Am I ready to explore a relationship with a woman?* he mused as he neared the Café. Not that he hadn't noticed women's eyes in the past, but then he was committed to God and the church. This was scary new territory for him, this fiery attraction. Never had a woman prompted such intense feelings.

His thoughts were interrupted by a voice from the opposite side of Main. "Joe, hey!" Jack Faulkner called, crossing the street to shake his hand.

"Hello, how are you?" Joe said. Their greeting transitioning into a hug. The two men had known each other since their boyhood in Lenox, Massachusetts, when Joe had been best friends with Jack's brother Robbie. It was a happy coincidence that led Jack to settle in the village, and shortly after leaving the priesthood, Joe had officiated at his wedding. A study in contrasts, the two men looked like Mutt and Jeff, Joe lanky and tall, Jack, medium height, broad-shouldered, and slightly younger.

"I'm good. Married life is treating me well, and the inn's booked solid all summer, so I can't complain. We're in the midst of hiring, so if you meet anyone interested in a job, please send them my way. You look great, by the way. The transition to layperson working out?"

Joe smiled. "It's been a process."

"Listen, Joe, while I have you. I know you've joined the practice with Pam Morgan and Elise. I imagine you're busy, but I wonder if you have time to talk to me?"

"Is this in a professional capacity? As a therapist? If yes, might you feel more comfortable with Elise or Pam? Sometimes distance can be helpful."

"Everyone knows everyone in this town. Have you forgotten that my wife's business partner is Pam's mother-in-law?" He referred to Lucy Morgan, his wife Lolly's friend and partner in a children's book business. "I'm really wanting to talk to a friend."

"Well, of course. I don't have my book with me, but when I get back to the office, I can check."

"Don't suppose you have any time today?"

"I'm free at five."

"I'll be there."

"First floor, all the way to the back. Door will be open."

"Thanks, buddy. See you later, then."

Joe resumed his walk to the Café at a brisk pace, realizing he was now late for his meeting with Murph and Greta.

Meryl found Rori in the dining room stacking menus when she arrived at Field and Fire. "Hey, girl!" the co-manager said.

"Where's Murph?" Meryl asked, gazing around at the quiet, empty space. They were planning to serve lunch during the summer months and had recently added a wide covered veranda that looked over the river for outdoor dining. Lunch had only been served on special occasions and holidays during the past winter, and they were still debating about extending into fall.

"He's meeting Greta and our hunky priest for lunch to discuss the wedding plans."

"Ex-priest," Meryl said drily. "Listen, Rori, if I were to duck out from about seven to nine tonight, would you be willing to oversee things?"

"Oh?"

Rori stopped shuffling menus and stared at her. As executive chef and co-manager, the two women held positions of equal stature, but on the occasions when Meryl was away, her friend and colleague took over as head chef, and Murph, as the other co-manager, assumed more responsibility. Thus far there had been little need for job switching, but Meryl predicted that with the kids here, she would be asking for a few nights off over the next few weeks.

"I'm actually having dinner with Joe at the winery tonight. That is if Wolfie gives us permission."

Rori raised an eyebrow. "I see."

"A friendly dinner."

"Uh-huh."

"What do you think?"

"About you dating the priest?"

"No, about covering for me."

"Of course. Ooh lah-lah, there'll be lots of disappointed village ladies if he goes off the market."

"Did you hear the part about friendly?"

Rori smirked, her dark brown eyes twinkling. "If you say so."

"Great, well, I'm going to head over to the winery and talk to Wolfie. Be back shortly." Meryl hurried out, forestalling further conversation about her dinner with "the hunky priest." As she walked the short distance down the gravel path leading to Morgan's Fire Winery, she reflected on the upcoming dinner and whether it was a good idea. She was very attracted to Joe and had been disappointed that he hadn't been in touch since the holidays. He was the first man for whom she'd felt anything for a long time. She wondered if she dared risk her heart again. Her musings were interrupted by shouting as she neared the winery. As she debated whether to wait until the argument ended, the front door slammed open and a red-faced Lyddie stormed out.

Slender and athletic, she was dressed for work in her black slacks and a crisp white shirt.

When the freckle-faced blonde spied her, Lyddie's face turned beet red. "Sorry."

Meryl smiled at her. "Everything okay?"

"Whole thing's stupid. See ya." Lyddie hurried off. *Clearly everything is not okay.*

Meryl pushed open the door to find Wolfie Morgan in the tasting room to the right of the lobby, pulling glassware out of cabinets, presumably preparing for a tasting. It was a beautiful room, the west wall like an old English library with mahogany woodwork. Glass-fronted cabinets holding glassware and hundreds of bottles of wine lined the inner wall. A wide cherry bar, its polished surface gleaming, sat in front of a dozen small tables, the east side of the room all glass, affording a spectacular view of the river.

"Hi, Wolfie. Bad time?"

"Nope. Got a group coming, but not for a couple of hours. What's up?" Richard Morgan's youngest made a perfect poster boy for the winery, with his long dark hair, thick beard, and piercing coal-black eyes

"How about tonight?"

He paused to give her a quizzical look. "Excuse me?"

"Is this room free tonight? I'd love to bring someone over for dinner."

He smiled. "Sure, it's free. I won't be around, though. Is that okay?"

"Of course. I'm just bringing a picnic basket over with everything. Might we use two glasses and grab a red wine? I'll settle up later."

"Take whatever you need. I'll alert Zeke and Cara you're coming, just in case they're wandering around."

"Thanks." She took a breath and then decided, *What the heck. He'll find out anyway.* "It's Joe...Joe O'Leary. Ran into him this morning, and we decided to have a dinner to catch up."

He grinned, the kind of grin that made women go weak at the knees. "Sounds great. I kinda thought you guys might have a thing a while back."

Meryl shrugged. "Just friends," she said a bit too quickly as her face grew hot.

"Whatever it is, I'm glad for both of you. He seems like a great guy, and any guy would be lucky to be with you."

"Flattery will get you everywhere," she said, giving him a silly curtsy. "Now I'd better get back to work. We'll be coming around seven thirty. I'm just taking a break, and Rori's covering. I'll bring the key, so feel free to lock up. I'll do the same when we leave."

"Have fun!" he called as she walked back through the lobby. "At least someone'll be having fun today."

When Meryl stepped back into the kitchen, Lyddie was in a heated conversation with Coco Flannagan, the pantry chef, who was shredding carrots over a huge bowl of fresh salad greens. Meryl passed by and heard Lyddie say, "It's time. We've been together over a year. Why can't he see that?"

"He's a guy," Coco replied as Meryl pushed open the door to her small office, closing it behind her. She was reasonably sure she'd hear the whole story by evening. There were few secrets in the kitchen. She didn't have to wait that long. She'd barely sat down when she heard a light tap on the door.

"Come in," she called.

Lyddie peeked in. "Do you have a minute, Chef?"

"Of course," Meryl said, standing and gesturing to one of two chairs on the opposite side of the desk. As Lyddie sat in one, she took the other. "What's up?"

"I just wanted to apologize for what you saw."

"No worries." Meryl gave her a warm smile.

"Can I ask your advice?"

"That depends. I'm afraid I'm no expert in matters of the heart."

"Wolfie and I have been together for over a year. I love him and I know he loves me. I think we should move in together, and he says no."

"Doesn't he live at the farmhouse?" Meryl asked, referring to Richard and Lucy Morgan's huge home less than half a mile south.

"Yes, but there's a gorgeous apartment above the winery. It was built for the manager, him, but he's never moved in. Says he likes Callie's cooking too much." Callie Richardson was the Morgans' cook and housekeeper. She'd been with the family for many years and had moved from Maine with them. "I thought I'd take a semester, maybe a year, off from Brown and move in with him, see how things go, but he says no."

Meryl sat silently listening, unsure of what to say. "So, you're at a standstill, then? Did he give you a reason for his decision?"

"He sounds just like my dad. Both of them say I'm too young and they don't want me to quit school, but I'm not quitting, just taking a break. Lots of people take time off."

"Sounds like they both care about you and want what they think is best."

"What do you think I should do? You've lived all over the place and done so much. Am I crazy to want to step back and take a pause to figure out what I want?"

"You're the only one who can decide that. My only advice would be to keep talking to Wolfie and your dad as you figure out what you want. There's probably no one right answer."

"Thanks, Chef," she said as she stood.

Meryl smiled. "My pleasure."

CHAPTER 5

"Hello!" Joe called, rising to greet the couple. The crowded Café was bustling with activity, but he'd secured a table in one of three quiet alcoves. Greta waved as they made their way across the room. *A handsome couple*, he thought, as they took their seats. Murph had wild curly red hair and caramel-brown eyes, tall and broad alongside his petite fiancée. Greta had soft violet eyes, her short, sandy hair cut stylishly to frame her oval face.

Murph draped his arm over her shoulders. "Hey, buddy, feels like months since we've seen you."

"Except every week when you stop by the house to pester him," Greta said, giving Joe a wink.

"No pestering, just checking in."

Joe laughed. "Well, whatever it is, I enjoy the company. How are you two?"

"Great," they said in unison.

"Shall we order, then we can chat?" Joe said.

"Why don't I go get the food," Greta said after they checked the menu and decided. "That way, you two can talk about the house and 'man stuff' related to the wedding." She rose and disappeared.

"You're a lucky man, Murphy O'Neill," Joe said as they watched her weave her way to the counter.

"Don't I know it."

"How's Daisy doing?" Joe asked, referring to their pet goat.

"Up to her usual tricks. She's a little escape artist. I've had to repair the gate about fifty times. She eats it!"

They chatted about odds and ends until Greta returned with their lunch on a small tray. Joe and Murph had ordered subs and Greta a beet and arugula salad. She also set three iced teas on the table.

"So, what did you decide? Are we still getting married?"

"You know it, babe!" Murph said, leaning over to kiss her temple.

They spent lunch chatting about details, mostly the use of the Friends Meeting House in Southport. Greta belonged to the Meeting and had gotten permission for the ceremony to be held there. The wedding was five weeks away, and they'd reserved the date. Next step was for Joe to meet with the clerk, which he promised to do in the next few days.

"I know Belle. A great person. Did she indicate that she would be there for the wedding?" he asked.

Greta nodded. "It's on her calendar."

"Would she like to participate, do you think?"

"That's your call. Murph and I are saying traditional vows. Would you be able to give us a copy ahead of time? If it's okay, we might like to change a few words, and then we want to memorize them and then echo each other. Are you okay with that?"

"Of course," Joe said, smiling. "I am a lay pastor now. There are no rules. You all set with the license?"

"Getting it next week," Murph said. "We've asked Darby and Seamus to do readings."

Joe nodded. "Great. So glad they're both coming."

"It means a lot," Greta said. "Particularly since I'm an only child. My Aunt Sarah's coming with my cousin, Ralph, but that's my only family."

"From what I can see, this whole village is your family and everyone else's," Joe said.

"Yes, we're lucky that way." She reached over to squeeze Murph's hand.

Joe regarded the young couple as he would a son and future daughter-in-law. In his first year as a priest, he'd been with the O'Neill family during the darkest period in their lives following the accidental drowning of Murph's six-year-old twin, Aislan. "Will you have people standing up with you?" he asked.

"I have Pam and Elise standing with me, and Murph has Sandy and his brother. We're not really calling them bridesmaids and groomsmen, but they'll help with seating and then stand beside us during the ceremony."

"Okay, then. Anything else?"

Sub long gone, Murph took a sip of tea. "As you may remember, we had planned to have the reception either at our house or my parents', but my best friend does not take no for an answer. Everything's set at Field and Fire, and my mom's making the wedding cake. Some old Irish fruitcake recipe she insists will be great."

Greta grinned. "Magical was her exact word."

"How delightful," Joe said, recalling several of Fiona O'Neill's creations over the years, usually redolent with spices and stuffed with raisins, candied fruits, and nuts.

"Except that it's a hundred proof," Murph said. "The restaurant's pastry chef's making another cake for those who don't wish to get soused eating a piece of whiskey-soaked fruitcake. There'll also be cookies and other desserts."

Joe laughed. "Well, it all sounds terrific. I'll meet with Belle and let you know how that goes. I apologize, but I have a client coming in ten minutes."

"Thanks, man," Murph said. "We've gotta get going too."

They parted outside the restaurant, Greta back to the high school, where she was a social worker, and Murph to Field and Fire. A warm breeze rustled the trees as Joe walked down Main Street to his office. The village was just waking up after a cold spring, with buds on the trees bursting open and flowering azaleas in early bloom. As he did every day, he thought about how fortunate he was to have landed here for this season of his life. He looked forward to this evening's dinner with Meryl and smiled. *Another new experience!*

~

"Calm down," Lolly Rogers Faulkner said as her husband paced in the cramped office of Merlin's Closet, the business she ran with her dearest friend and partner, Lucy Morgan, wife of Richard. Jack liked things orderly, so he rarely visited the cramped office with its mountains of boxes and books. His wife's partner, Lucy, was hidden at her desk pretending not to listen.

"I'm trying, but this is crazy. She wants to drop out of college. They barely know each other. For Christ's sake, she's not even twenty-one!"

"If you fight with her, she's just going to dig her heels in."

Jack sat hard on a stack of boxes, a defeated expression on his ruddy, handsome face as he ran his fingers through his thick sandy-brown hair. Finally, he looked up and grinned at his wife of four months. "I'm an ass, aren't I?"

"No," she said, bending to kiss the top of his head. "Just a concerned dad."

"Wait'll Cynthia finds out," he said, referring to his ex-wife and Lyddie's mom. "She'll fly down here and blame me for the whole mess."

"It's not a mess," Lolly said, pushing strands of raven hair from her forehead. A full-figured goddess was how he referred to her, and he wasn't far off. Her violet eyes stared down at him, love shining in them. "It's not a mess, is it, Lucy?"

"Don't get me involved in this," a voice called from behind the wall of books.

"You really need a bigger space," Jack said, glancing around at his surroundings. "Why don't you start looking? We might even be able to build something out at Barnum's Ledge."

"My husband's been nagging me about the same thing," Lucy said. "We already store tons of books in the barn, but it's nice to have a space in town. That way we can walk to lunch and the garden. We love being in the middle of village life instead of out at the farm."

"What do *you* think about your stepson and my daughter?" he asked.

"I love Wolfie and Lyddie, but if pressed, I'd say they're both young in their own way. However, I'd never say that to either of them."

"Exactly! Maybe Joe will have some ideas."

"You've talked to Joe about this?" Lolly asked, eyes registering surprise.

"I made an appointment to see him later."

"Oh... Well, good. Then you'd better let Lucy and me get back to work."

Jack kissed her, waved over the books in Lucy's direction, then departed. After the door closed, Lolly came around to the side of the desk. "Always something, huh?"

"Yup. If I had to guess, the last thing on Wolfie's mind is settling down. I have no doubt that he's fond of her, but between running the winery and finishing school, he's got a lot on his plate. I heard that Lyddie was trying to get him to move into the empty apartment at the vineyard, but I think he's happy with us right now."

"Yeah, just observing them together, it does seem she may be a bit more into this relationship than he is. I mean, he is a major heartthrob. Who wouldn't want to move into his wolf den?"

Lucy laughed. "Let's get back to work and leave young romance to sort out itself."

CHAPTER 6

Joe headed home after his chat with Jack Faulkner. He wasn't sure he'd helped much, but at least the concerned father had had space to vent. After showering, he dressed and grabbed a nice bottle of wine he'd been saving for a special occasion. He was pretty sure Meryl would have selected wines, but he wanted to offer something. Then, on his way out, he had a better idea. He went back into the house and rummaged through Murph's cupboards until he found an old, wide-mouthed bottle, which he wiped off and filled with water. Grabbing a pair of scissors, he went out to the gardens and fields surrounding the house and filled the makeshift vase with a colorful assortment of wildflowers. Satisfied, he set the bottle on the floor of his truck, inside an empty pail with rags to prevent it from tipping over. He then put the scissors on the doorstep and headed out.

As he drove into the winery lot, he spied Meryl coming down the path from Field and Fire. She held a large basket in one arm and waved with the other.

"Hello," she called. "You're early. I was hoping to set up before you arrived."

Joe smiled, stepping out of the truck with his bouquet. "Apologies. I'm happy to help, or I could sit in the truck till you're ready?"

"Of course not, come on!" she said, waiting for him to reach her.

"For you, milady," he said, holding out the flowers. "I was going to bring wine, but then thought these might be a better choice."

"They're beautiful, thank you," she said, setting down her basket to give him a hug.

Only a brief, casual embrace set his body aflame. "Can I carry your basket?"

"I've got it. You bring your beautiful flowers."

He followed her in, gazing around. "Quite a place they have here, isn't it?"

She'd shed her chef's coat and wore denim capris and a peach-colored blouse, its neckline revealing a hint of cleavage. A simple silver necklace, bracelet, and earrings were her only adornment.

"It is. Billionaires do things right."

"You look pretty tonight."

"Not like a kitchen drudge who's been slaving over hot stoves for the past three hours?"

He smiled, reaching forward to brush strands of her sandy hair from her forehead. "Not at all." It was an intimate gesture, perhaps more intimate than he'd intended, but he wasn't sorry. He noticed her cheeks reddening. "I'm sorry, was that too forward of me?"

"To echo you—not at all. If we're being honest, there's an attraction here, even if neither of us is ready to act on it."

"Yes," he said, standing very still, meeting her sky-blue eyes.

Meryl smiled, patting his arm. "Something for us to talk about during dinner?"

She turned away and began unpacking the basket.

"What can I do?"

"Why don't you choose a wine? We are having crispy duck, mushroom risotto, and a green salad. Whatever you think might complement that. I have some cheese and olives for appetizers. Please grab two wineglasses as well."

"I feel like a kid in a candy store," he said, opening one of the glass-fronted cabinets. "Any rhyme or reason here?"

"That cabinet's mostly reds, which would be my preference. If you prefer a white, the refrigerated cabinet at the end is full of choices. There are only a dozen of each wine because Wolfie stocks these cabinets for tasting. There are cases more downstairs. I promised we'd reimburse him for anything we consume."

"The wine is on me," he said, turning to open the cabinet behind him. "How about this pinot noir?"

"Perfect. That's always my choice with duck."

Joe uncorked the wine and let it rest, wandering around as Meryl set up the food. A few minutes later, she brought the cheese and olives to a table by the window. "Shall we start here? With a glass of wine and some cheese?"

Joe grabbed the wine and poured two glasses, handing one to her. "Cheers," he said, as they faced one another.

"Cheers," she said softly, a shy smile on her face.

"Thank you for this."

"My pleasure."

They talked about this and that, gazing out at the water, its surface choppy and fast-moving in the growing twilight. They'd been talking about the restaurant when Meryl said, "Aren't we lucky?" her voice soft and pregnant with emotion. "I've lived in several parts of this country and abroad, but this is truly the most beautiful place I've ever called home."

"You have a nice spot on the harbor side, don't you?"

"Gorgeous. I'd buy it in a heartbeat if Carl and Mattie Ferguson ever agreed to sell."

"So, you're settling in, then?" The waning light played across her face, her eyes like pools of moonlight.

Her expression registered surprise. "Yes... I guess I am. Aren't you?"

"If I'm being completely honest, I'm not sure at this point. I'd like to say yes, but I've seen so little of the world. I've thought about volunteer work overseas if they would consider a fifty-year-old geezer like me."

"You are hardly a geezer, Joe O'Leary," she said, flashing her beautiful smile.

"Thank you for saying that. On the subject of our mutual attraction, however, I'm afraid I may be too old for you."

"Well, I'm telling you you're not. Like half the women in the village, I am, indeed, very attracted to you. Your age is one of my favorite things about you."

"Now I know you're kidding."

Meryl slid off her high stool and came around to his side. She reached up, draping her arms around his shoulders. "I'm not kidding, and I would very much like to kiss you."

As warning bells sounded, Joe smiled, wanting nothing more than to sweep her into his arms. He waited for what seemed like hours, then opened his legs and drew her body between them, leaning down to capture her luscious lips. Meryl responded as the kiss deepened and their tongues found each other.

Breathless, his emotions churning, Joe pulled back first. "Haven't done that since I was a young man. Before I entered seminary."

"Oh?"

"Much better than I remember."

"I'm glad." She reached around to stroke his lean, strong jaw, her touch light and gentle. "And before this goes any further, I'd better see to dinner."

Sated, Joe leaned back in his chair, patting his flat, hard stomach. "This is the most incredible meal I've ever had, picnic or otherwise."

"Well, that is high praise from someone who has clearly been wined and dined by many over the years."

"Well deserved praise."

"I brought small desserts. Tiny flans, barely a mouthful. Do you think you can fit one?"

Joe laughed. "I'm sure of it! Can I help with cleanup?"

"Not at all. You sit and enjoy the moon on the river."

Later, their flans a distant memory, Meryl had packed everything back in her basket and was writing a note for Wolfie when Joe came up and wrapped his arms around her from behind, kissing the back of her neck then resting his chin on her shoulder.

Meryl nestled back against him. "Mmm, that's nice. Looks like you've worked through the I'm-too-old-for-her nonsense."

"Not entirely, but great food, several glasses of excellent wine, and your precious company have softened that concern a bit."

She turned to face him, her blue eyes gazing up, brimming with emotion. "I'm glad."

Joe grinned. "By the way, remember to let me know what I owe for the two bottles of wine." As he spoke, his hands found her waist and drew her closer. Close enough so she could feel his erection pressed against her.

"Are you coming on to me, Joe O'Leary?"

His grin widened. "I believe I am, although I haven't the faintest idea what I'm doing."

"Could've fooled me," she said, moving her hips, body caressing and stroking him.

As they kissed again, Meryl realized every inch of her was alive with sensation, every fiber of her being wanting him. As his hands moved down to caress her breasts, her breath came in gasps. "Oh boy," she whispered as his hand slipped under her blouse. "Are you sure about this?"

"If you are," he said, gazing down at her with his beautiful dark eyes.

"Not the ideal place for it," she murmured into his chest, knowing that she would throw her clothes off in an instant if he asked.

As she spoke, a sound came from the lobby and a voice called, "Hello!"

"Oh gee," Meryl said. They broke apart, and she smoothed her blouse. "It's Cara, I think."

Seconds later, Cara Feldspar, the assistant vintner, stepped through the door. Medium height with long blonde hair draped in a braid over one shoulder, she was dressed in sweats and what appeared to be slippers. "Hey, guys, sorry. I was doing my rounds. I forgot. Wolfie said you were *eating* in here."

Her pointed reference to the word eating irritated Meryl, who was technically her senior. The twenty-four-year-old apprentice had always seemed rather cheeky, even to Wolfie, with whom she'd flirted when she first arrived. "We're just packing up," Meryl said. "No need to stay. We'll lock up."

"Sounds good," Cara replied, but she continued to stand in the doorway, staring from one to the other of them.

Meryl forced a smile. "I'm not sure if you've met Joe. Joe O'Leary, Cara Feldspar, assistant to the vintner."

"Hello," Joe said, stepping forward to shake her hand.

"Well, hello," she said. "I've heard about you. Haven't you done a few bartending gigs at the restaurant?"

"I have."

"Is that your profession? Bartending?"

Joe smiled, sensing the tension from the woman behind them. "Among others."

Meryl cleared her throat as she came to his side. "Well, we don't want to keep you, Cara."

The younger woman smiled, flipping her braid off her shoulder. "That's considerate, thanks. Great to meet you, Joe. Night." She turned and strolled out, disappearing into the shadows on the opposite side of the lobby.

"Insufferable woman," Meryl whispered, looking up at him.

Joe laughed, his arm circling her shoulders drawing her to him. "Pretty little thing, and doesn't she know it?"

Meryl waved her hand in dismissal. "Let's not allow her to spoil our evening. Although with her lurking about, we may want to save our amorous encounters for another time."

"Amorous encounters? I like the sound of that," he said, leaning over to kiss the top of her head.

"You've gotten quite comfortable with amour even if you're so old and decrepit."

"Ha-ha. Can I carry your basket back to the kitchen?"

Meryl leaned into him, loving his strength and warmth as he held her. "Yes, I believe you can."

They walked slowly, arm in arm, along the path to Field and Fire. When they drew close, she stopped. "I had a wonderful time tonight."

"Me too."

"Can we do it again, maybe someplace less public?" she said.

"I would love that. You tell me. Your schedule is much busier than mine."

Her fingers caressed his chest as she planted soft kisses on his long, strong neck. "Let me see what things are like once the hellions arrive tomorrow. I must be crazy to have said yes."

Joe drew her closer, kissing her deeply before they stepped apart. "Of course. I'll look forward to anything."

Meryl groaned with the wrench of separation as he bent, picking up the basket and handing it to her. "Good night, Joe."

"Good night," he said, kissing her forehead. "I am sad to be leaving you, but I'll console myself by anticipating next time."

"Me too." *Back to the fray*, she thought as she turned away, praying she would not find chaos on the other side of the restaurant's back door.

CHAPTER 7

At eight Sunday morning, Sherry Stockdale roared in, beeping the horn of her enormous neon-yellow Humvee. Meryl looked out the upstairs window facing the driveway and shook her head. She wondered if her nitwit half sister was planning to shove her kids out the door and take off.

"Good Lord," she said aloud, heading downstairs to greet them. "Here we go."

By the time she opened the front door, the kids had alighted, both carrying duffels and rolling suitcases. Gigi's luggage was pink, as was her wardrobe: shorts that barely covered her ass and a tank top. Her blonde hair was tied back in a sloppy ponytail looked as if she'd just rolled out of bed and hadn't looked in a mirror. Her skinny redheaded brother wore cut-off jeans and a Red Sox T-shirt, a baseball cap backward on his head.

"Hi, guys, welcome!" Meryl called, coming down the front steps. She received grunts in reply, her attempts to embrace them largely rebuffed. Not so with their mother.

"Hey, Merylie, long time no see!" Sherry rushed forward to hug and kiss her. While the two women were roughly the same height, Sherry towered over her in six-inch espadrilles. "You are such a life saver!"

"My pleasure. Come in, everyone."

"I can't stay long 'cause Rodge is waiting at the marina as we speak."

Meryl followed them into the house, wondering how her sister's shoes would do on a boat, not to mention her skintight denim shorts and purple, midriff-baring camisole. "Kids, why don't you throw your bags by the stairs, and I'll show you your rooms after Mom leaves. Come in and have something to drink." As they stepped into the kitchen, she turned to Sherry. "So, you leave tomorrow?"

"We do," she replied, plopping down on a stool at the counter. "The owner's chomping at the bit to get his fancy new boat. He's paying Roger extra to make the trip in three days instead of five."

"I thought you'd be away three weeks?"

"We will. The guy knows nothing, or should I say less than nothing, about sailing. Zero, zip. Rodge has to teach him everything and also help him hire a crew."

Meryl listened to the woman she barely knew rattle on about yachts and their travel plans as the kids wandered out to the porch and sat on the glider to stare out at the river. *I'm sure they've heard it all before*, she thought. One of those people who abhor a conversational lull, Sherry never let anyone get a word in edgewise. Finally, after fifteen minutes, she hopped off her stool. "Well, hate to drop 'em and run, but we're on a really tight schedule. Put them to work and let them help you. It's actually better if you keep them busy, if you know what I mean. Idle hands and all."

"Anything I should know?"

"Naw. They're good kids and pretty independent. They make friends real easy. Lemme say goodbye, then." She hurried out to the porch, and Meryl could hear her fussing and cooing, telling them to behave. She thought she heard Gigi beg her mother not to leave them, but her plea was met with a "pooh, pooh, don't fuss. This is the first real vacation Mommy's had since you guys were born. Now, be good!"

She reappeared and grabbed her gigantic purse from the counter. "Meryl, you are a peach. I'll call when I can, but we may be incommunicado for at least a week. Have fun!" With those words, she breezed out, slamming the door in her haste to be gone.

Meryl stood in the kitchen, stunned. After a few minutes, she went out to the porch to find two dejected kids as dazed as she was. "You guys hungry? Can I fix you something?"

They shook their heads, then Kip said, "Mom stopped at McDonald's on the way."

Real food, I meant, Meryl thought. *Poor kids.* "Well, then, it's a beautiful day. Too chilly for swimming, but I thought we might walk on the beach or take a ride around town to orient you?"

They shrugged.

"Okay, think about it. Would you like to see your rooms?"

They followed her upstairs with their belongings. There were three bedrooms, all wood-paneled. Meryl's was the largest on the water side, with a wide picture window and small bathroom with a tub. Two smaller bedrooms on the street side shared a bath. She'd brought her own linens and bedding to the rental.

Kip's room had a dresser, a queen-sized four-poster bed covered with a colorful patchwork quilt, each square a different print, and a small writing desk. The quilt was the first Meryl made in a quilting class she'd taken the year before she went abroad. Gigi's room was furnished with a double-sized iron bed painted a soft sage green with a star quilt in shades of pinks, pale greens, and blues. A small dresser stood in one corner, painted to match the bed, and two end tables. Each room had a small closet as well as rows of pegs for hanging clothes running the length of one wall.

"They're small, but the beds are comfortable," Meryl said. "I'll let you settle in, then we can decide how to spend the day."

"I thought you worked at the restaurant," Kip said.

"Not today. We're closed Sunday and Monday." As she spoke, Meryl thought she might have glimpsed disappointment in their eyes, perhaps because they hoped to have the house to themselves?

What have I gotten myself into? she thought, descending the stairs. It was just after nine, so she grabbed a coffee and her book and headed out to the porch. As she passed by her phone on the counter, it lit up, and she saw she had a text from Joe. *How's it going?*

She took the phone to the porch. *They're here, hiding in their rooms. That's all I know so far.*

She was about to set the phone down when he texted: *Want reinforcements? I'm free this afternoon.*

Yes, please! she wrote back. *Lunch is on me.*

12:30 okay?

Yes, she replied thinking, *That's why I love you, Joe O'Leary!*

JOE KNOCKED ON HER DOOR SHORTLY AFTER 12:30. MERYL OPENED IT TO find him smiling. "Sorry, the village traffic was murder."

She laughed, stepping aside. "I'll bet. Come in."

After introductions, they decided to take Meryl's car, which she pronounced safer and more comfortable than the truck.

"Couldn't we ride in the back of the truck?" Kip asked. "It's only a rinky-dink town, so we won't be on the highway."

"People have accidents even in rinky-dink towns," Meryl replied.

They took a quick drive down Main Street, then out to the Point past Cove Inn and Spa and Land's End, the vast farm owned by Rex and Faith Miller. Faith was one of the Darn Yarners group along with her sisters, Hope and Grace, as was Mavis LaSalle, owner of the exclusive event venue and spa.

"Look at the horses," Gigi cried as Meryl turned the MINI Cooper around at the Point and drove by the Millers' fields. "They're beautiful. I love horses."

Joe turned around in his seat to face her. "Do you ride?"

"I have a few times, at camp."

"There's a Loop Trail that rings the entire village. It's a really popular horseback riding path, as well as walking and running," he said. "Maybe we could find someone to take you out."

"Really?"

Meryl looked over at him, her eyes wide. "Do you ride?"

He smiled. "A little. Used to ride more as a boy. How about you?"

"The villa where I stayed for most of my time in Italy had horses. We rode back into the hills. It was lovely."

"I bet it was," he said, casually draping his arm over her seat.

Very cozy, she thought, sitting up straighter. "So, I thought we'd eat at Field and Fire. I have lots of possible lunch choices. Then we can walk across the fields to Morgan's Fire and see the stables. There's also a path to the beach, if you'd like to go down to the river. We can see what we feel like doing."

"Sounds great to me!" he said.

No response from the back seat.

CHAPTER 8

No one was around at Field and Fire when they arrived. After eating warm bacon and Gruyere cheese sandwiches on day-old baguettes, which Joe proclaimed to be "the best thing I've ever tasted," they walked over to the winery. Wolfie was setting up for a wine-tasting, but he paused to chat. The kids seemed enthralled and hung on the dark handsome vintner's every word.

"He's pretty cool," Kip said as they headed back to the restaurant.

"He's hot," Gigi sighed, gazing back over her shoulder.

"Yes, very hot," Meryl said, exchanging looks with Joe. The couple walked behind them, occasionally holding hands, their bodies brushing against one other. Her breath came in gasps as she recalled his arms around her and his hands on her skin as he slipped them under her blouse. *Get a hold of yourself, girl!*

As they near the kitchen door, Rori drove up and parked her orange Bronco in the side yard. She hopped out and approached them. "Hey, guys, what's happening? You must be the visiting niece and nephew? I'm Rori. I'm way cooler than those two, so if you need help finding fun things to do, call me."

Meryl shook her head, smiling at her colleague. "Rori, this is Kip and his sister, Gigi. We're having a tour."

"How'd you get roped into this?" Rori said, gazing over at Joe, who had just released Meryl's hand.

"I volunteered."

"What are you doing here on your day off?" Meryl asked.

"I forgot my backpack last night. It's got a few things I need, including my fitness tracker. In a moment of craziness, I signed up to go hiking with the group from Cove Yoga."

"That sounds fun. I've seen their flyers at the center and have been wanting to check that out," Meryl said.

"They're a nice bunch of people, I hear. This is my first hike, but I know some of them from yoga. You probably do too."

"Well, I think we're going to take off. I made us lunch from the kitchen." She turned to her companions. "I'll just grab my bag and meet you three at the car, okay?"

As Joe, Kip, and Gigi walked to the Cooper, she followed Rori inside. As soon as the door closed behind them, Rori turned to her. "Cute kids. They don't look like terrible monsters."

"They've been here for three hours. We have three weeks to go."

Rori grinned, grabbing her backpack from a hook near the office door. "I'll make you a list of fun ideas."

"Thanks, oh cool one. I didn't cook, just warmed things up, so everything should be off."

"So... I'm more interested in what's cooking with you and our gorgeous ex-priest."

"Don't refer to him that way," Meryl snapped, her tone a bit rougher than she intended.

"And there's nothing cooking. We're friends."

"Uh-huh."

Meryl smiled. "Well, maybe we're exploring more."

"There will be many broken hearts in Horseshoe Crab Cove," Rori said. Meryl slung her purse over her shoulder, and they walked out together.

"Don't be ridiculous."

"I'm not. You can't believe how many women I know who have future plans for him."

"Goodbye," Meryl said, her hip nudging Rori's. "Have fun on the hike."

"You too!"

She turned to her three companions, who were leaning against the Cooper. "I thought you suggested walking to the stables from here," Joe said.

"Of course... Yes, I did!" Meryl said, throwing her purse into the car. "Shall we?"

A warm sunny day, there was a gentle breeze coming off the river as they strolled along the path that led from Field and Fire to the Morgans' farmhouse and stables. Occasionally, a grouse or pheasant flew up from the tall grass, and the cries of gulls reached them from below.

"This is a great walk, isn't it?" Joe said. "I haven't been this way before."

"Where are we going?" Kip asked. He had pocketed his cell phone, which he'd been glued to all through lunch, but his hand kept reaching for it in case things became unbearably monotonous.

"We're going to say a quick hello to Richard and Lucy Morgan, who live in the farmhouse, then we'll take a peek at the stables before walking down to the beach. Sound good?" Meryl had phoned the Morgans earlier and asked if they'd mind a visit. She'd been quickly assured that they would be most welcome. "You know who else lives here? Wolfie from the vineyard."

That seemed to perk them up a little as they reached the crest of the hill where an ornately carved bench sat. Teak flowers and leaves trailed over its back and down its strong, sturdy legs. A small brass plaque on the front edge of the seat was nestled between a cluster of vines and read: *Laura Morgan, beloved wife and mother: "Cross the meadow and the stream and listen as the peaceful water brings peace upon your soul."*

"Laura was Mr. Morgan's first wife and Wolfie's mom," Meryl explained before turning to Joe. "They brought this with them from Maine. She's the Laura of the community garden."

"Must've been quite a woman," Joe said as they began their descent to the stables, barns, and farmhouse.

"Yes."

"He's a lucky man. Lucy's wonderful too."

Kip and Gigi had run ahead and disappeared around one of the barns. When they caught up with them, the kids were talking to Weezie Morgan, the youngest Morgan daughter. Weezie ran the pony camps and gave lessons to kids and adults. Petite and strong, she had her dark curly hair stuffed under a baseball cap, and her chocolate brown eyes danced with light as she greeted them.

"Hi, Weezie, I hope we're not disturbing you," Meryl said.

"Of course not! Welcome! Hi, Joe, good to see you too."

"Likewise," he said.

"So, have my niece and nephew introduced themselves?" Meryl asked. "They are Kip and Gigi. They're staying with me for the next three weeks."

"How fun. Where do you guys live?"

"Nowhere for long," Kip replied, frowning, "but we're living in Northport right now."

"Gigi was just telling us how much she loves horses," Meryl said. "Any chance we might be able to come out for a ride sometime?"

"Of course, anytime. You know, another two-week pony camp starts tomorrow. There's still space. It runs from nine to four. The kids learn to ride and work on the farm grooming the horses, mucking out stalls, lots of fun stuff. We also leave time for arts and crafts because I love that stuff. I've got a great group starting tomorrow."

Meryl turned to her niece and nephew. Gigi looked ready to burst, and even Kip appeared interested. "What do you think guys?"

"Are they our ages?" he asked.

"This group has kids from ten to fifteen. The older ones help the younger ones. It's fun."

"Sounds great. Kip? Gigi? What do you say?"

"Yes!" she cried, jumping up and down.

"I guess it'd be okay," he said.

"Terrific," Weezie said, turning to Meryl. "Kids bring their lunch.

If they forget, they can always run up to the house and our housekeeper Callie'll make 'em something. Of course, you'll get the family discount. We can settle that later. Right now, it's important that I do a quick assessment of their riding ability. The other campers went through their assessment last week. I just want to start thinking about pairing riders to horses and decide if we need to borrow horses from Land's End." She gazed down at their feet. "Not the best shoes for riding, especially yours, Gigi. You look close enough to my size. I'll grab a pair of my old boots from the barn."

"You mean you want them to ride now?" Meryl said.

Weezie chuckled. "Just around the corral. Not long. Have you got time?"

"Of course, we do," Meryl said. Weezie turned and disappeared into the barn.

"Are you guys sure about this?" Meryl said, amazed at the opportunity that had fallen into their laps.

Both kids nodded. They all wandered toward the nearest corral, which was empty. Beyond the enclosure were large, fenced fields, where a number of horses grazed. "This place is awesome," Kip said, eyes wide.

Meryl exchanged a smile with Joe, who had been listening quietly throughout the entire eye-opening exchange.

When Weezie emerged from the barn, she held a pair of boots and helmet in one hand and a lead in the other, a beautiful brown horse with a star on its forehead following her, all saddled up and ready to ride. "This is Piccolo. She's a gentled mustang, probably closest in breed to a quarter horse. She's our gentlest stable horse now, even calmer than our domestic, farm-raised horses."

Weezie handed Gigi the helmet and boots, which she pulled on immediately. "How do they feel?"

"A little big."

"We'll go to Bayport and get some boots later," Meryl said. "Do they need real riding boots and special clothing, then?" Meryl asked.

"Jeans are good, and sturdy boots a must. Work boots are fine. They don't need riding boots at this level."

"Great. We'll take care of it. Should we get her a helmet too?"

"No, we have a tack room full of training helmets. They're the basic skull caps, and we have them in all sizes. The crew and I will fit them tomorrow morning, no worries."

Joe had taken hold of Piccolo's lead while the women talked. The kids were petting the horse's nose.

"Okay, then," Weezie said. "Who'd like to go first?"

"Me!" Gigi cried as she moved to the horse's side.

"Allow me," Joe said, lifting her like a feather and depositing her in the saddle.

Weezie went around the horse to secure Gigi's feet in the stirrups. "Since you're already in the saddle, we'll let you stay there and have Kip learn the right way to mount his horse."

"Oh, gee, I'm sorry," Joe said.

"Just kidding. They have all day tomorrow to learn," she said, as she took the lead and headed toward the corral gate.

Twenty minutes later, Gigi reluctantly dismounted to allow her brother his turn. As Weezie instructed him how to use the mounting block, Richard and Lucy Morgan appeared, walking arm in arm. "Hey, folks, welcome! We're so glad you found your way. Is my girl showing you a good time?"

Meryl smiled, walking over to greet their hosts. "She's invited the kids to join tomorrow's pony camp. She's assessing their riding now."

"Wowee, that's great. Why didn't I think of that? Hey, Joe, how're you doin'?" Richard said, turning to shake his hand. Closer in age to Joe than the others, the tall, slender family patriarch had thick salt-and-pepper hair and prominent, bushy eyebrows that added warmth and animation to his handsome, craggy features. Like his youngest daughter's, his dark brown eyes shined with warmth and mischief.

"Couldn't be better," Joe said, returning Richard's firm handshake, then reaching out to Lucy.

"Hello, Joe. You're looking well," she said, beautiful as always in faded jeans, turtleneck, and a pale blue Morgan's Fire sweatshirt.

"Thank you. You as well."

"My Pammie says you're settling in at the office. She and Elise are so pleased to have you there."

"They've been wonderful, Andy too. Couldn't ask for a better work environment."

The group stood talking and observing as Kip and Weezie worked in the ring. Gigi had run off to get a closer look at the horses down below. Finally, Kip dismounted and Weezie pronounced him ready to go.

"Would you all like to come up to the house for a drink? Lemonade? Iced tea?" Richard asked.

"Hot tea or coffee?" Lucy added. "The breeze is getting chilly."

"Thank you, but we'd better get back. Especially since we've still got to go clothes shopping for pony camp," Meryl said. "Weezie, I can't thank you enough. You'll let me know what I owe you in the morning?"

"Of course."

They called Gigi back, said their goodbyes, and started up the hill to the path. "What a place," Joe said, marveling as he always did at the incredible home and farm that Richard Morgan had created in a few short years.

Meryl reached out and took his hand. "Like heaven, isn't it? Full of generous, kind people."

CHAPTER 9

Joe came along on the shopping trip to Bayport, where Meryl succeeded in purchasing Kip and Gigi boots suitable for riding and a pair of jeans to supplement the one pair each had brought with them. It was almost six when they exited the mall, so she suggested they eat on the way home at the Brickyard Diner, a small but popular eatery midway between Bayport and Horseshoe Crab Cove. When Joe raised an eyebrow in surprise, she laughed. "It's one of my favorite spots for breakfast, and they have the best burgers. Who doesn't love a burger once in a while?"

All of them ordered the house special burger, Gigi with the special sauce on the side. The enormous plates were also piled high with curly fries. "Wow!" Gigi exclaimed when they arrived. "These are much better than McDonald's."

The adults sat side by side across from them in a booth, occasionally holding hands under the table. Joe's libido soared whenever Meryl was near him. He had thoroughly enjoyed the day with her and the kids.

"So, kids," he said, setting down his half-eaten burger. "How have you enjoyed your first day in Horseshoe Crab Cove?"

His mouth full of food, Kip shrugged, but Gigi said, "It's been awesome. I mean, I think we both expected boring," she added, dragging out boring, "but it's been great." She suddenly looked over at Meryl, who was frowning. "What's the matter, Aunt Meryl? Are you pissed that we're here?"

Meryl smiled, shaking her head. "No, nothing like that, but I just thought of something. We haven't asked your mom if the pony camp's okay. Should we call her? I'm not sure when they were setting off, but they might still be in cell phone range."

Kip rolled his eyes. "She won't give a shit."

"Watch your language, son," Joe said, his voice low and steady. He received a scowl in return.

Meryl looked over at the two. "Let's call Mom. Would one of you call her now? Just a quick call in hopes we'll catch her."

Gigi pulled her cell from her back pocket and punched in the number. "Hey, Mom, it's me. Yeah, everything's cool. Aunt Meryl wants to talk to you about us going to pony camp. We're super excited. What? Yeah, she's right here." Gigi handed the phone to Meryl, who stood and pointed to the door, mouthing *I'll be right back.*

She asked Sherry to hold while she exited the restaurant, then said, "That's better. We're eating dinner at the Brickyard and it's noisy. Sorry to bother you."

"No prob. We're on the boat, but still at the dock. Leaving at four in the morning. So, what's up?"

Meryl gave a quick description of their day and the invitation for the kids to join the pony camp, ending with, "It's all happened so fast, and as we were eating, I suddenly thought I'd better check with you to see if you felt okay about it."

"Yeah, I guess. That does sound fun. Wish I could've taken them."

"It's a great program, and they can meet some kids from the village. The farm at Morgan's Fire is amazing."

"Billionaires row, from what I hear." Sherry's voice sounded pouty and resentful.

"Well, you're their mom. What do you think? They did fine when Weezie, the director, assessed their riding ability."

"Yeah, they've both ridden before," she said, lowering her voice to a whisper. "Mickey, two boyfriends ago, had horses. He was always having them out to his ranch."

"So, you're okay with it? They seemed pretty excited."

"Who wouldn't be? Yeah, of course. It's fine. Keep 'em busy. Listen, I'm getting the hairy eyeball from Rodge, so I've gotta go. Hug the kids for me."

"I will."

"Thanks, Meryl. Don't mind me. I'm really grateful the kids are with you."

"My pleasure. Bye, Sherry. Safe trip."

When she returned to the table, she gave them the thumbs-up. "She had to go, but she sends her love."

Kip rolled his eyes, but couldn't quite hide his smile, and Gigi jumped up and down, clapping her hands.

"Who has room for dessert?" Meryl asked. "We can get something here or stop at Cove Creamery in town?"

They all voted for the Creamery, and after settling the bill, they headed out.

After ice cream cones enjoyed in the community garden, they drove back to Meryl's sated and happy. The kids ran up to their rooms to prepare for pony camp and Meryl walked Joe to his truck. As he turned to say goodbye, she placed her hands on his chest and sighed. "Thank you for today. I couldn't have done it without you."

He smiled, a warm loving smile. "Yes, you could have, but it was fun for me."

"Having you there made it fun for me too."

His fingers played across her cheek, smoothing errant strands of hair from her forehead. "They seem like good kids."

"Time will tell. You know if you keep that up, I'm going to jump into your arms right here, damn the consequences."

"Well, we can't have that, now can we?" He leaned down and kissed her forehead lightly.

"So, when can I see you?" she asked. "Tomorrow's my day off."

"Unfortunately, I have clients all day. I'm free from noon to two, though, if you'd like have lunch? Sandwiches from the Café and eat in the garden?"

"Lunch sounds great, but I'll bring the food. Is there anything you don't eat?"

"Liver."

Meryl laughed, a throaty, robust laugh that he loved. "Well, then no liver sandwiches. Shall we meet in the garden at noon?"

"Perfect." He bent to kiss her, lightly at first, but when she responded, the kiss deepened, lips opened, tongues entwining.

Finally, she stepped back, breathless.

"Not in front of the kids, right?" he said.

"Ha-ha, see you tomorrow," she said. With another quick embrace, she headed up the front walk, turning to wave as he pulled out.

No question about it. I'm in love with you Joe O'Leary, but what in the world are we going to do about it?

CHAPTER 10

The previous evening, they had come home after supper and retreated to their rooms with phones and tablets. After checking their preferences, Meryl had made and packed sandwiches, drinks and fruit, placing two small canvas cooler bags in the fridge. She puttered around, planning what she might make for Joe's and her lunch, then decided to head up for a shower and her book. Just before retiring, she stopped in first to Kip's room, then Gigi's. She seemed animated and excited, him less so.

"Are you looking forward to camp?" she asked him, and received a shrug in return. "You don't have to go, you know."

"I know," he said, staring at the floor. "I want to go. Could be fun."

"And if it isn't, you don't have to keep going."

"Thanks, but I have to keep an eye on Gigi."

"Did your mom ask you to do that?"

He guffawed, rolling his eyes. "Hardly. My dad... Your dad. He made me promise."

"But you weren't more than four, were you? Do you even remember when he died?"

"I was five. I remember, and I promised. He knew our mom was useless. Everyone did."

"That's a big burden for you, honey."

He shrugged. "Gigi's a good kid. Never any trouble, unlike me."

"Oh?"

He smiled. "I'll tell you when we know each other better."

Meryl reached over and hugged him. "I'm gonna hold you to that. Night."

MERYL DROPPED THE KIDS OFF AT MORGAN'S FIRE. WHEN SHE WALKED away, Gigi was already engaged in conversation with two other campers. Kip hung back, but Weezie had assured her that they would get him involved right away. Once home, she turned her attention to lunch for Joe and herself. She decided upon mushroom baguettes since she had several bags of fresh mushrooms in the fridge and some great French bread. She sautéed the mushrooms, then transferred them to a covered bowl. She would reheat them and assemble the baguettes just before she left for town.

After trading her Birkenstocks for sneakers, she headed out for a walk. She loved the walk to the end of Beach Road onto the Loop Trail. It was quiet, and she rarely failed to see at least one familiar face. Today, she came upon Sandy and Pam jogging. They appeared to be returning home at the end of their run.

"Morning, Meryl!" Pam called, waving as they slowed down and paused beside her.

"Hi, you two," she said, marveling as she always did at the beautiful couple, so clearly in love and happy. Pam's strawberry-blonde hair was pulled back in a ponytail, and she wore sweats and a T-shirt, the top's colors bringing out the blue in her eyes. Her gorgeous dark-eyed companion was in shorts and a singlet, his long dark hair stuffed under a Field and Fire baseball cap.

"So how are you making out with the kids?" he asked. "Have they short-sheeted the bed and wrecked the place yet?"

She shook her head. "No, they've been really good, actually. Kind of shocking. So far, we've been keeping them busy."

Her boss gave her the eye. "We?"

"Joe kindly came along on our adventures around town yesterday. We stopped at the restaurant for lunch."

"Joe, huh?"

"Yes, and don't read anything into it. It was kind of him, and we had a great day." She turned to Pam. "The best part was that your sister invited them to join Pony Camp for the next two weeks. It's a godsend, and I hope they like it. I've been a little freaked out worrying about how I was going to entertain them."

"Joe, huh?" Sandy said again.

"Would you stop!" His wife poked him. "Have a great day, Meryl!" With that, she urged him forward, and they resumed their jogging. Their spectacular waterfront house, designed and completely rebuilt by Sandy, was only a short distance from her rental and had amazing river and bay views.

Lost in thought, Meryl walked farther than she'd intended and was surprised to see the time upon her return. She quickly assembled the sandwiches and threw fruit, cookies, and bottles of iced tea and water into a picnic basket, then ran up for a quick shower. She'd have to hustle to make it to the community garden by noon!

Joe's morning was busy with clients and paperwork. He had arrived an hour early to dive into the piles of mail and invoices on his tiny desk, but had barely made headway sixty minutes later. Andy had introduced him to his assistant, Karen Miller, who took care of the accountant's billing and insurance paperwork, but he had yet to find time to meet with her. *Tomorrow*, he told himself. He made a note to phone Karen, switched on the electric teapot, and set the papers aside to wait for his first client, Martha Brewer. Martha had been one of his parishioners at St. Mary's, and he was a little nervous about the appointment. For myriad reasons, he had not encouraged his former congregation to seek him out for counsel and advice. Mostly he didn't want to step on Father Flynn's toes.

As he sat ruminating, he heard footsteps in the hall, then a light tap on the door as she peeked around the corner. Joe stood and went to shake her hand. "Welcome, Martha. So good to see you." About his age, she had reddish hair streaked with gray, pale blue eyes, and a handsome freckled face etched with the years. Married to a brute of a man, she'd often sought Joe's counsel as her priest.

"Hello Father Joe," she said, beaming up at him.

"Can I get you something to drink? Tea? Water?"

"A tea would be perfect," she said, as she gazed around the office. "Wonderful space you have here overlooking the gardens. Lots of possibilities."

He smiled. "The unruly gardens that I keep telling my associates that I'm going to tame." He held out a basket of tea bags, and she chose English Breakfast.

"A spoonful of honey, if you have it," she said, as she settled into one of the easy chairs. Joe couldn't be sure, but it almost appeared that she batted her eyelashes at him.

"Just boiled," he said, setting a mug of tea, spoon, and honey jar on a small table next to her. He grabbed his tea mug from the desk, topped it off with hot water, and came to sit in the other easy chair.

Martha stirred in a generous spoonful of honey, then rose to set the honey and spoon on a napkin next to the teapot. "Cheers," she said, raising her mug as she sat again.

"How have you been?"

"You know... Life with Eddie is never easy."

"Is that what you've come about, then?" he asked.

"Sort of...partially. Well, yes, I'm thinking of leaving him. Finally. The kids are grown, and I'm tired of taking care of everything while getting smacked around in between. Getting too old for it."

"Have you talked to Father Flynn?"

"There's nothing more to say."

As a priest, Joe had been obliged to discourage divorce, but as a lay counselor, he was no longer bound by church doctrine. In truth, he had often found it difficult to encourage people like Martha to stay in abusive marriages, when no amount of counseling was going to change their circumstances. Eddie Brewer was a bully, a nasty alcoholic bully. "I can't say I'm surprised, nor will I counsel you to stay, if you're sure?"

"I'm sure. I'm planning to live with my sister, Loretta, in Northport for a while till I get my bearings. The house we live in is Eddie's family home, and I want no part of it. Loretta's house is very close to my work, which is good." Martha was an OR nurse at Saint Elizabeth's Hospital in Bayport.

"Does Eddie know?"

"Not yet. That's why I wanted to talk to you. What do you advise? Lorie thinks I shouldn't tell him, just pack up while he's at work."

"Is that what you think?"

"Well... After twenty-six years together, I'd like to be aboveboard, I'm just... Well, I'm afraid he'll...that he might..." Her voice trailed off, and her eyes filled with tears.

"You're afraid he'll hurt you."

She nodded. "Yes."

"Perhaps you could have someone or a few someones with you when you tell him?"

"Oh, would you, Father... I mean would you, Joe?"

"I was not necessarily suggesting me. Perhaps Father Flynn could be with you?"

"No! I mean... Jonathan's a good priest, but he's not my friend like you are."

Joe swallowed, considering his next words. There was the issue of barging into Father Flynn's spiritual community, but there was also the issue of Martha herself. Over the years, the abused, lonely woman had sometimes flirted with him, seeking more than a spiritual relationship with her priest. "I want to be supportive, but as your therapist, I'm not sure this would be appropriate."

"I just said you're my friend!" Her raised voice sounded shrill and desperate.

"This is a counseling practice, Martha. We have a professional relationship."

"I'm talking about the past two decades of friendship."

"Priest to parishioner," he said gently.

She shrugged, her face scrunched in a scowl. "I hear you've been dating."

"Martha, this isn't appropriate, I'm sorry."

"Surely you know I've been madly in love with you for as long as I can remember. I was hoping we'd be able to date once you left St. Mary's, and next thing I know, you're dating someone down here."

Joe gazed at her, his eyes reflecting compassion and sadness. "Is this why you came to see me?"

"What do you think? I'm leaving Eddie for you. I certainly don't wish to wallow at Loretta's house for the next chapter."

"Martha, this is a professional office where I see clients who need counseling. I don't take social calls here."

"Then where? Could we go to dinner sometime soon?"

"I'm sorry, no."

"Why not?"

"For many reasons. Perhaps the most important is that I was your priest, and this isn't appropriate. I also don't have the kind of feelings for you that you deserve. Never have, never will."

"Why?"

"Martha."

"The gossip mill was right on the mark. You are seeing someone. Who is she?"

"I'm going to stop the conversation here and recommend that you seek another counselor if you need support in leaving Eddie."

"Well, screw that." She stood up, nearly upsetting the little table holding her mug of tea. "How much do I owe you?"

"Nothing."

"Fine. Thanks for nothing. Have a nice life with your bimbo, whoever she is."

Before he could utter another word, Martha stormed from the office and slammed the door.

Joe sat back in his chair and sighed. *Not as if I didn't see that coming,* he thought.

CHAPTER 11

Two clients later, Joe closed his office door and headed across the street to the community garden. He looked forward to seeing Meryl, but the earlier encounter with Martha Brewer had left him shaken. Leaving the priesthood had been a decision about which he was sure and confident. It was right for him. However, he hadn't anticipated the reactions of some of his former parishioners and wondered again if staying in the area was the best way to forge a new life for himself. As he walked through the garden gates, he resolved to shrug off the morning and stay in the present with Meryl, of whom he was already very fond.

He spied her on the eastern end of the garden, sitting on a bench in the sun. She waved, her face lighting up with her beautiful smile. This was real, he was sure of it.

"Hello," he called, passing a half dozen gardeners tending their plots.

"Hello yourself." She patted the bench beside her. "Is this okay, or would you prefer another spot? Everyone seems to have their favorite garden bench and view."

"My favorite is wherever you are," he said as he sat down.

"What a sweet thing to say. Did you rehearse that?"

Joe laughed. "No, but it sounded pretty good, didn't it?"

"Yes, it did."

"And it's true. I'm glad to see you, Meryl. It's been a strange morning."

"Oh?"

"I'll tell you, but first, how did camp drop-off go?"

"Very smoothly. They seemed to get right into the group. Gigi more than Kip, but Weezie was headed for him when I left and promised she'd pair him up with some friendly campers."

"And insist they all get along, if I know her."

"Yes, she's a force, isn't she? So, tell me about your day so far."

"All's fine. I'm enjoying my work even if I'm finding some unanticipated consequences of leaving the church and staying local. It's a bit awkward at times. A fresh start might have been wiser for me and my former parishioners." Without breaking the confidentiality of the counseling session and not naming names, he gave her a summary of the awkwardness of his time with Martha Brewer.

"These are small towns, and everyone knows everyone else's news, and you're big news. A handsome bachelor of a certain age who's suddenly available. That's like wow!"

"Ha-ha."

"Face it. You're the season's bachelor of the year. It'll die down."

"I hope so."

Meryl opened the picnic basket. "So, I brought grilled mushroom baguettes and iced tea. Sound okay?"

"Perfect."

They sat chatting and eating as they observed the activity in the garden. Now over three acres, more raised beds had been added so that thirty-five lucky gardeners had their own plot to tend with five left over as community beds for flowers, herbs, and whatever people wanted to grow and share. "Have you a plot?" he asked as he watched a couple weeding.

"No, but I'm on the waiting list. In the meantime, Rori and I are planting a kitchen garden behind the restaurant. I also asked Pam about adding some flower and tomato beds on the east side."

"Pam?"

"She's the unofficial floral and plant designer for Field and Fire. She does an incredible job. She won't care what we do, but I want to check with her anyway."

"She's an amazing person, isn't she?"

"The best. From what I hear, my boss was quite a wild man, but he's certainly settled down now that he's with Pam."

"Perhaps it was just the business he was in? That night club?" He referred to Sandy's, a music venue her boss had started and run for many years. The property overlooked the ocean north of town, and Sandy had sold it for millions. It hadn't taken him long to find his next investment, the quieter but wildly successful Field and Fire. In the meantime, Sandy's was still going strong, attracting big-name and local musicians to its seaside building that hung over the crashing waves of the Atlantic.

"Maybe," she said. "He was married to Lolly, and she's no wild woman."

They ate and chatted about this and that. Occasionally, one brushed an arm or a hand against the other in the intimate way of couples. It was a totally new experience for Joe, and he loved it. Meryl's touch both soothed and aroused him in ways he'd never imagined. The time flew, and it was with regret that he said, "My next client will be here in about an hour, and I did want to show you the office before we part. That is, if you have time?"

"I'd love to see it," she said. They tidied up the remains of their picnic.

"Those cookies were incredible," he said, brushing crumbs from his khakis.

"Moon and Stars. One of the best bakeries around. We buy all the bread for the restaurant from them and occasional desserts. Their cookies, and all their baked goods for that matter, are out of this world. Our pastry chef admits that she can't top some of their tarts."

Joe laughed as he stood. "I usually try to avoid bakeries as I tend to overbuy, but I'll have to stop in."

"It's deadly."

"Can I carry your basket?"

Meryl paused, then smiled up at him. "Thank you, that would be nice." As she handed it to him, their fingers interlaced for a few seconds, and she blushed. "I won't tell you what I'm thinking right now, oh Bachelor of the Year."

Joe gazed down at her. "Probably the same thing I am."

THEY CROSSED THE STREET, AND MERYL TOLD HIM TO LEAVE THE BASKET on the porch. They stepped inside, the front parlors dark after the bright sunlight. As her eyes adjusted, Meryl peered around, spying one woman waiting in the east parlor. Joe nodded to the stranger, leading Meryl down the hallway to his office in the back.

"That's the waiting room for all of us."

"It's very attractive. Did you have a hand in the décor?"

He chuckled, reaching forward to unlock his door. "Hardly. I'm color blind, and the parlors were furnished years ago by Andy, I believe. Maybe my colleagues upstairs have added a few touches."

"Was that your client waiting?" she whispered.

"No, mine's not due until two thirty. Here we are," he said as the lock gave way and he opened the door.

"What an inviting, comfortable space," Meryl said. Joe closed the door behind them. They stepped into the warm interior with its view of the backyard gardens. The room was furnished with a few side tables that flanked overstuffed armchairs, a kilim rug, small corner desk with a two drawer file cabinet to one side, and a Victorian love seat covered in faded navy brocade.

"It's a work in progress, eclectically furnished with attic finds and a few purchases. I'm still intending to have a go at the gardens this spring."

"Looks like this old Victorian had formal English gardens at one point."

"You think?"

"I do. It must have been beautiful. I like wild gardens with profusions of blooms rather than neat rows."

"Me too."

"I'm happy to help with the weeding and restoring, if you'd like."

Joe smiled. "I would. Do you have time for tea?"

"I'd love a cup, if you do? Have time, I mean."

"Of course," he said, turning to the teapot. "Help yourself to a tea bag. All the mugs are clean."

A few minutes later, they sat side by side on the love seat, sipping tea. Joe had pulled one of the side tables in front of them, set with two napkins and a small ramekin and spoon in case they wanted to discard their tea bags. "This is perfect," she said, gazing out at the garden. "If I were your client, I would feel quite comfortable here."

Joe set his mug on the table and turned to her. "If you were my client, I couldn't do this," he said, fingers gently tracing her jawline. "You are so beautiful."

Meryl set her mug beside his. "Thank you," she said softly, reaching to hold his hand. "You are too."

They moved closer, and her arms circled his shoulders as he drew her to him. "I haven't done this since my teens, and even then, my experience was very limited."

Her hand stroked his strong jaw, fingers light and gentle. "I think we should do as much or as little as we want and not rush things till you...till we are feeling at ease."

"Is that possible, do you think?" He leaned in, capturing her lips in a searing kiss that left them both breathless.

"Is the door locked?" she whispered.

"Better check." He slipped out of her arms and went to the door. "Now it is." As he spoke, Joe gazed down at her half-recumbent figure, loving every inch of her. One arm behind her head, she looked relaxed and peaceful, unlike the butterflies fluttering in his chest.

Instead of sitting back down, he moved the table aside and sat on the kilim covering the floor in front of the love seat. He patted the space beside him. "I had this professionally cleaned and I bought a nice, thick rug pad. I guarantee it's much more comfortable than that sofa."

"Well, this is a surprise," she said, slipping off the love seat and into his arms. "You never cease to surprise me, Joe O'Leary."

Wrapped around each other, he kissed her again. Meryl responded, moving against his lithe, strong body, feeling his erection like a lightning bolt. As he moved his hands to her breasts, tentatively at first, then slipping beneath her T-shirt, she moaned, waves of desire coursing through her. "Oh, it's been so long since I've been touched, and never like this," she murmured, moving her hips against him.

"I'm glad," he whispered in a husky voice she'd never heard him use.

Meryl unbuttoned his shirt and caressed his strong, hard chest. "You're in great shape for an ex-clergyman," she said, her eyes playful as she met his.

"Clergymen keep in shape."

"Oh?"

"So we're ready for times like this," he said.

He unhooked her bra and cupped her breasts, his fingers teasing her nipples to hard, ripe buds. Meryl found herself rising to a rolling, exquisite orgasm that left her gasping for more. Maneuvering slightly, she pulled off her bra and T-shirt, then opened his shirt wider to trail kisses down his chest. Joe rose and removed the shirt. "Are you sure about this?"

"What do you think?" she replied, fingers moving down to unzip his slacks and release him.

As she began to slip out of her capris, he reached down to inch both her capris and panties down her legs. As garments flew across the room toward the windows, she whispered, "Have you protection?"

He smiled. "I have. In a crazy moment of intention, I stopped into the pharmacy in Southport." He bent to kiss her, then his lips and tongue moved down her neck to her breasts, taking one then the other in his mouth.

"Oh Joe," she moaned as her hips writhed in the ecstasy of another release.

Gently, he parted her legs, and his fingers delved tentatively, then deeper inside her. Meryl guided him to her clit, almost blind with wanting him. Suddenly, he withdrew and reached for his khakis. After slipping the condom on, he gazed down at her. "Are you ready, sweet girl?"

"I'm hardly a girl, but I've never been more ready in my life." As he shifted his body between her legs, she grasped him, guiding him, hungry for him.

WHEN HE SLIPPED INTO HER WARM, WET DEPTHS, JOE KNEW THE SWEET perfection of a longing fulfilled. He thrust deeper as her hips rose to meet him. "Meryl, my sweet, beautiful girl," he whispered as they began an intense dance of passion, her legs wrapped around him, her hot center enveloping him, welcoming him to come deeper and deeper. Several minutes later when they reached a thunderous, simultaneous climax, he thought, *Home. I've come home.*

After they lay wrapped together, drenched in sweat, he gazed down, kissing her nose. "Thank you for the most amazing few minutes of my life."

Meryl smiled. "I hope there will be more. It was amazing for me too. At this moment, I feel absolutely perfect."

"I'm glad," he said, planting a light kiss on her forehead, then lips.

"By the way, after all your talk about inexperience, you were pretty deft with that condom."

He grinned, his face reddening. "I practiced."

"Oh, do tell," she said, playfully kissing his chest, then looking up into his beautiful soft eyes.

"First with a banana, then, you know."

"As I said, you are a man of many surprises."

"Thank you. I wouldn't want to be totally predictable."

Her hands cupped his face. "That, you will never be."

They suddenly heard talking from the hall, and he reached up to grab his watch. "Oh, gee, it's two twenty and this client is always early."

Meryl smiled. "Likes to squeeze a few extra minutes out of you, does she?"

"Something like that. I'm afraid we have to end this precious interlude." Groaning softly, he pulled out of her warmth and gathered their clothes. As they dressed, there was a rap on the door and a voice called, "Hello! Mr. O'Leary, are you in there?"

"Just be a moment," he called.

"You know she's going to smell sex all over this office, don't you?" Meryl whispered as she pulled up her khakis and fished her shoes out from under the love seat.

"Really?" Eyes wide as saucers, he gazed around.

"Have you got any room spray?"

"Actually, I do, because I allow a couple of clients to smoke during sessions." He opened the drawer of his desk, extracting a small plastic spray bottle, then circled around, spraying liberally as a tart, citrusy scent filled the room.

"Hmm," Meryl whispered, feigning exaggerated sniffs. "Might fool her."

"Ha-ha," he said, stowing the spray and crossing the room to embrace her. "I'll miss you, my sweet."

"We'll find a way to do this again soon, I promise."

As they kissed, another call of *yoohoo* came from the hall. Reluctantly, Meryl pulled out of his arms and surveyed the room. "Looks okay... Just like before."

"Let's hope so."

"How public do you want this to be?"

He met her eyes. "Hmm... What do you think?"

"I think it might be best if I slip out the window into the garden. Is there a way to get out back there?"

"Yes, but that's ridiculous." Joe watched her crank open one of the large casement windows.

Window wide open, Meryl turned and beckoned with one finger. "One more kiss, Romeo?"

He grinned, stepping forward. "I'll be in touch. Good luck with the kids today."

"You're welcome to come for supper."

"I can't, even though I'd love to. I'm eating with the O'Neills. We're discussing the wedding."

"Bye, my sweet," she said, caressing his strong cheek before she spun around and hopped out the window into an unruly rose bush. "Ouch!" Joe watched until she extricated herself and hurried toward the gate. Before she rounded the corner, he waved, then cranked the window shut. *What will Joan think?* he wondered, then realized that at this joyful moment, he didn't really give a damn.

As he crossed the room toward the door, he suddenly spied a piece of the shiny condom wrapper under the love seat and grabbed it, opening his tiny trash can lid and tossing it in.

"Well, well, what have you been up to, Mr. O'Leary?" Joan Richmond said as he opened the door and she sashayed by him, scanning the room.

What indeed? Joe thought, then inquired if she wanted tea.

"I'd like to say I'll have what she had, but I fear that's not on the menu," she said, plopping down on one of the easy chairs.

Oh Lord, he thought, turning to make the tea. *What will the town make of this?*

CHAPTER 12

Meryl drove into Morgan's Fire shortly before four, waving to Richard as she passed the farmhouse, and parked near the stables. Several parents stood near the fence, watching as their kids cooled down their horses. Kip and Gigi were nowhere to be seen. She spied Weezie directing three campers as they brushed their mounts. "Hey, Meryl! They're in the barn. Great day!"

Meryl strolled into the barn, pausing as her eyes adjusted to the dimness. There were two rows of stalls. Hearing laughter from the far row, she headed down, where she found Kip and two boys about his age joking as they brushed their horses. No Gigi. Not wanting to disturb the guys, she retreated and walked the length of the first row. She discovered Gigi and three other girls lounging in the fresh hay of an empty stall, chatting. "Hey, Aunt Meryl!" she said, sitting up. "These are my friends, Cara, Rachel, and Leanna."

"Hello," Meryl said, smiling at the group. "Don't want to disturb you. I'll be outside when you're ready."

"Sure thing!" she said, turning back to her friends.

Meryl headed back outside, where she found Weezie talking to a short, stocky man with sandy hair and rosy cheeks, dressed in work pants and a green Morgan's Fire Stables T-shirt. She'd seen him before, but they had never been formally introduced.

"Hey, Meryl, do you know Gus? He's the boss here. He manages the horses and all of us."

"Gus, hello," she said, extending her hand, which he took. "I knew I'd seen you before. We used to be neighbors, right?"

He nodded. "My family just moved from our rental on Beach Road to our new house a few months back."

"You're not too far from the restaurant, are you?"

He smiled. "As the crow flies. Our driveway's off the main road, just before the winery and Field and Fire turnoff."

"Lucky you."

Gus smiled, his green eyes twinkling with warmth. "We sure are. If you ladies will excuse me, there's something going on in one of the mustang enclosures. That much dust can't be good."

They watched him hurry off to the east corrals. "We just got three new mustangs," Weezie explained. "They're beauties, but still skittish and feisty. It's tough when they come from different herds." As she spoke, she scanned the corrals where her campers were finishing up.

"I'd love to hear more about them sometime when you're not busy."

"We'd love to show you. You can take Gigi and Kip anytime. They're all set."

"How'd it go?"

"They did great. Made friends right away. Jumped right into things. They're great kids."

"Thanks so much, Weezie."

"It's our pleasure. Sorry, I've gotta help that group," she said, pointing to the nearest enclosure. "See you in the morning!" She waved over her shoulder as she ran off.

The kids chattered happily all the way home about their day, their horses, and their experiences trail riding. "Gus and Dennis are awesome," Kip said. "They matched everyone to the right horse. It's like a gift."

Meryl smiled, listening to her nephew in awe of Gus and his assistant, both of whom were known as equine whisperers for their close, instinctive ways of interacting with horses. Richard Morgan had lured Gus east from his brother's stables to assist with the startup of the Morgan's Fire stables, but then Gus had asked to stay when his wife's mom, who lived in Connecticut, was taken ill. According to anyone who'd watched him work, Gus was a marvel with a wild horse, one of the best in the business.

"And Weezie's cool too! She took us on a long trail ride. Did you see us? We passed pretty near the restaurant when we cut through the fields."

Meryl shook her head. "Darn, I missed you, but I've been home and in town most of the day."

"We get to work with the wildies too!" Kip said.

Meryl swallowed hard. "Oh? As part of camp? I didn't realize."

"He's exaggerating," his sister said. "We spent some time watching them. A couple came up and let us pet them. They're beautiful."

"Yes, they are. They're also unpredictable and dangerous. I'm sure your mom wouldn't want you too near them."

"No worries!" Gigi said, her tone light and breezy.

No worries, indeed, Meryl mused as they pulled up to the cottage and the kids piled out.

"Hey, Auntie, there's a note!" Gigi called from the front stoop.

Now I'm Auntie, she thought, coming to read the note her niece handed her.

It was from Frankie Brown, her neighbor. It read: *I wonder if you and your houseguests would like to have a simple supper tonight? It's your day off, I believe. Six-ish? Frankie, next door.*

How incredibly kind of her, Meryl thought as she unlocked the door. "Kids, we've had an invitation to dinner next door. Okay by you?"

"At the hobbit house?" Kip asked.

"The very one."

"Oh, can we, can we?" Gigi asked, her eyes pleading.

Laughing, Meryl opened the door. "You two head in and I'll call Frankie to see if I can bring anything."

~

Just after six, the three walked next door, and Gigi knocked on the "hobbit door," which was opened by their tall, lanky neighbor. Dressed in denim overalls and red-and-white-striped T-shirt, Frankie wore her curly salt-and-pepper hair held back by a bandana, her blue eyes sparkling with warmth.

"Welcome, come in!"

She led them through a rabbit warren of rooms to a wide deck over the river, half of it screened in. The screen doors were open, and a row of cushioned chairs and odd wicker pieces were scattered around. A long dock stretched out over the river, where several crab nets and buckets hung on poles along its length.

Meryl had never had dinner with Frankie, but the two women had enjoyed drinks several times on one another's deck. She enjoyed her neighbor's company immensely and always felt comfortable in her cool little house, where knickknacks, books, paintings, and treasured possessions covered every surface.

The kids took one look at the dock and Kip said, "Can we? I mean the crab nets?"

Frankie smiled. "That's what they're there for, kiddo." As the kids ran off, she turned to Meryl. "Drink? I'm having red wine, but I have most everything."

"Wine would be perfect. Thank you for doing this, Frankie."

"My pleasure. I have to get my kid fixes where I can, through my friends' grandkids and nieces and nephews."

"Can I help with dinner prep?" Meryl asked as their host brought the wine and two glasses to the screened-in porch area.

"All set. Mulligan stew, salad, and a nice crusty loaf from Moon and Stars."

Meryl nodded as Frankie handed her the wineglass. "Oh, how delightful! I haven't had Mulligan stew for ages."

"Everything in the kitchen plus peas!" they said simultaneously.

Frankie sat beside her on a soft, lumpy, but comfortable sofa, gazing out on the river and the kids' efforts to net the crabs that skittered along the sandy bottom. "It's one of my specialties since I'm kind of a lazy cook. I've observed that most kids like it."

"I'm sure they will," Meryl said after taking a sip of the delicious wine.

"It's rather intimidating cooking for a master chef, so I thought I'd better not be too experimental."

"Nonsense. I love all kinds of food."

As the kids played, catching crabs, releasing them, and dangling their legs in the water, the two women chatted about village life and their funky waterfront neighborhood. Meryl sighed. "This is so relaxing, watching the river, isn't it? Have you lived here long?"

"Over forty years. Like a couple of my dear friends, I came to the village to heal, found this little boathouse, made it livable, and have been here ever since."

"You're lucky. I've moved around a lot."

"So does this feel like it could be home?" Frankie asked.

"It's beginning to. I love my job and my little cottage. Wish I could buy it. I've begun to make good friends, too, which is nice."

"Makes all the difference. My friends are very precious to me."

"Can I ask you something Frankie?" The other nodded, regarding Meryl with kind eyes. "Do you know Joe O'Leary?"

"A little. What I know I like. He's been here for years, but mostly based in Bayport. I tend to stay close to home."

"You're not Catholic, then?"

Frankie chuckled. "No, although my dear parents would disagree. I'm a Quaker and have been for many decades. My ex-husband, Leonard, was a birthright Quaker. He got me started. I attend the Hampton Meeting with my dear friend and fellow yarner Helen Winthrop, or occasionally the Meeting in Southport. Tell me about Joe."

Meryl swallowed, gazing out at the kids, who were now hanging upside down, heads almost touching the water. "Is that okay, what they're doing?"

Frankie smiled. "Worst that can happen is they fall in. They do know how to swim, don't they?"

"I think so. I hope so."

"It's low tide."

"Good." Meryl took a deep breath. "So, you asked about Joe. We've been... Well, we've seeing a bit of each other."

"How nice."

"Why do I get the feeling you're not surprised?"

"I saw you two together last New Year's Eve at the farm. It seemed as if there might be a spark."

"There was, but since then we haven't seen much of each other, what with my work and him establishing his counseling practice. We reconnected recently. It's been wonderful."

"I'm happy for you, my dear."

"Thank you. Truthfully, I can't help but worry that it's all foreign territory for him, and I've not exactly had the best of luck in my love life."

"So, you'll figure things out together."

"No advice?"

"Oh dear, you're asking an old hermit here. Leonard and I married very young and grew apart relatively quickly. Except for a few gentlemen friends over the years, my relations with the opposite sex have been sparse, I'm 'fraid."

"Love is tricky, isn't it?" Meryl said, watching the kids laughing and playing, feeling glad she'd agreed to have them.

"Yes, it is, but when you find it, you are fortunate."

"Yes," she said, smiling at their host.

"What do you think? Shall we have supper before they launch themselves off the dock and we lose 'em down river?"

"Great idea. How can I help?"

CHAPTER 13

Fiona MacGregor O'Neill greeted him at the door with open arms. "Joseph O'Leary, as I live and breathe! We haven't seen you for months! Where have you been keeping yourself?"

Joe returned her warm embrace, especially welcome after another weird session with a former parishioner. Like Martha Brewer, Joan Richmond openly flirted with him at the same time, chiding him for leaving the priesthood for a "life of sin." Joan had gone on and on with an endless string of complaints about him abandoning his flock. While she admitted that she liked Father Flynn, she moaned and groaned, saying "things just weren't the same." Again, Joe wondered if he'd made a mistake making his new home and beginning his practice so close to St. Mary's.

He hung his jacket in the front hall. "It's been a busy time, setting up house, establishing my practice, and—"

"A budding new romance, I hear!" The writer and farmer with flaxen hair and deep green eyes winked. "Don't look so surprised. The parish grapevine picks up news with lightning speed, and you haven't exactly been discreet. Holding hands in the community garden, canoodling at the winery. Not to mention a tryst in your office? Come in and say hello to Murphy. He's just come in from the fields."

As if on cue, Murphy Senior, a big hulking man with florid cheeks and a thick head of red hair streaked with gray, stepped into the front hall, extending his hand, the only part of him not covered with dust. His jeans and shirt were streaked with brown, mud and dirt caked at his knees and elbows. "Hello, my boy. Good to see you lad. I'll just pop upstairs to clean up and be down in a tick. Fiona's probably told you, the kids are on their way."

"Good to see you Murphy," Joe said, shaking his hand.

"Come back and get a drink," his hostess said, leading him through the parlor to the kitchen.

As he followed Fiona, he braced himself for yet another interrogation by a former member of his congregation. The O'Neills were friends, but somehow, he didn't think he'd escape the grand inquisition.

"Wine? Beer? What can I get you, dearie?" She held a bottle of red wine in one hand, white in the other, both unopened.

"Red wine would be great, unless you're opening the other."

"Red it is. It's a warm evening. I thought we'd have our drinks on the terrace."

"Sounds perfect." He took the colorful charcuterie board with its assortment of cheeses, meats, fruit, olives, and vegetables, and followed her out the back door to a shaded terrace, its large irregular flagstones punctuated with patches of moss, herbs, and grass. He set the board on a wrought iron table. "You've outdone yourself. This platter is a work of art, Fiona."

"Everything excepting the olives and the St. Nectaire and Camembert cheese was grown or raised right here on the farm." The O'Neills raised goats and a few cows as well as all manner of exotic herbs, vegetables, and fruits. With three large greenhouses, they gardened year-round.

As Joe admired the spread, Murph Junior's truck pulled into the yard, and he beeped.

"There they are!" Fiona said, waving. As Joe went down to meet the young couple, she flew back into the kitchen for white wine and beer.

"Hey, Joe," Murph said, embracing him. Greta came around the truck to follow suit.

"Good to see you both," Joe said, perhaps a little too emphatically.

"Oh, jeez," Murph said. "Fiona's giving you the third degree, isn't she?"

Joe smiled. "Not yet. Perhaps your arrival will put it out of her mind."

"Sorry, I should have warned you, man. She's been getting intel about you and Meryl from several of the local busybodies. Now she's dying to hear the real story straight from the horse's mouth."

Greta patted Joe's arm. "Don't worry, we'll try to steer the conversation toward the wedding or some other topic."

Murph rolled his eyes. "Good luck with that."

Between the three of them, they managed to deflect Fiona's inquiries during the cocktail hour, and her husband refused to allow her to interrogate Joe during their dinner of lamb shanks, new potatoes, and farm greens. After his "leave the man be" edict at the start of the meal, she knew better than to continue pressing their former priest.

Finally, as they enjoyed their coffee along with warm bread pudding topped with vanilla ice cream, Fiona said, "I know my family has forbidden me to ask questions about your love life, but am I allowed to ask—are you happy, Joseph?"

He smiled, setting his fork down, considering his next words. "I am happy in my new profession and my home. I made the right decision a year ago. I'm just questioning whether Horseshoe Crab Cove is the best place for me to live and work. It may be too close to my old life and hard for my congregants to adjust. I don't want that for them or Jonathan Flynn or myself."

Eyes wide, Fiona stared at him. "You're not thinking of moving away?"

Joe shrugged. "I'm not sure what I should do. As you've heard, I've been seeing Meryl Stockdale. She's a wonderful person, and I'm very fond of her. I'm afraid our relationship may cause her unpleasantness if certain restaurant patrons make the kinds of comments I've been hearing this week."

"I can't imagine that would happen," Fiona said.

"Mom, what planet are you living on? You think the Martha Brewers and Joan Richmonds aren't going to take digs at Meryl if they have the opportunity?"

"No, I do not!"

"Even if they don't, this transition is a bit bumpier than I anticipated," Joe said.

"Maybe take a trip?" Murphy Senior suggested. "Have you ever taken a vacation?"

Fiona rolled her eyes. "Says the man who's never taken a day off in his life."

Greta, who had been listening quietly, turned to her fiancé. "Maybe your dad is right. If Joe takes some time off to travel and have some fun, maybe people will have time to adjust in his absence?"

Joe nodded. "I may, indeed, go away, but I'm considering a retreat. It was suggested to me when I was stepping down last year and I wasn't interested then. I think I am now. Perhaps I'll do the retreat, then travel a bit, figure out next steps?"

"Where would you go?" Greta asked. "On retreat, I mean."

"There's a nondenominational retreat center in southern Maine. It's a great place. I would have to apply, see if there's an opening. I'd also have to inform my newly established clients that I'd be taking a break. And no worries, I would be back in plenty of time for the wedding."

"And maybe suggest that any former parishioners among them find another therapist?" Greta said. "That's a very reasonable request."

They talked awhile longer, then Joe said good night. As he drove home, he thought about the conversation and the prospect of leaving Meryl for such an extended period. On the one hand, it made him sad because he was already deeply in love with her. On the other hand, everything had happened so quickly. *Maybe a cooling off period would be helpful?*

CHAPTER 14

Tuesday flew by as Meryl continued to worry about how she would juggle responsibilities at Field and Fire with Kip and Gigi's activities. One of the camper's dads had offered to drop the kids at home today, but what about tomorrow? Even if she took a few days off here and there, it was going to be a lot of juggling.

After much research, Sandy had decided to take Field and Fire in a whole new direction, necessitating huge changes to the menu. His vision involved adding extensive offerings for vegans and vegetarians, and Meryl had been working on recipes for months. Now she was busy breaking in a new entremetier or vegetable chef.

That evening, her prayers were answered when Lucy and Richard Morgan came to Field and Fire for dinner. When she stopped by the table to say hello to the couple, they asked how she was, and she mentioned how grateful she was for Weezie extending the invitation to join pony camp.

"They're having a ball," Richard said. "I stop by to see what's up three or four times a day."

"Or more," Lucy said, winking at Meryl.

"Or more. I'd be a camper myself if they let me. Anyway, your two look like they've lived here all their lives. Both seem to have lots of buddies."

"I'm glad," Meryl said. "Now to figure out what to do with them after pony camp. They're old enough to be on their own, but I hate to leave them every night."

"What about my Amy?" Lucy said. "She's taking a semester off from college. She just got back from four months in Arizona, working on Richard's brother's ranch in Saguaro Valley. She's looking for things to do, and I'm sure she'd love some extra money. In fact, we've been encouraging her to apply here to waitress, but so far, she's resisting. She loves sitting, though."

A call to Amy that evening had her signed up for camp pickup and some afternoons and evenings. Meryl planned to take time off during the kids' final week, so suddenly, the visit seemed manageable. Joe called Wednesday to say hello, but seemed preoccupied, and they ended the conversation after five minutes. On Saturday, he called to ask if she and the kids would like to go on a picnic Sunday, and she accepted.

Shortly before noon on Sunday morning, the four of them set off from Meryl's, strolling down Beach Road toward the Point. At the road's end, they turned south, walking along a path that followed the cliffs, with several grassy areas on the water side. Some of these small open spaces had trails that led to the rocky shore. The kids ran ahead, backpacks with towels and a change of clothes bobbing against their backs. Joe carried an overstuffed pack holding their lunch, and Meryl a smaller pack with her towel, a light quilt, and ginger cookies she'd made that morning.

"How was your week?" he asked.

"Busy. The restaurant's been crazy, and then there's those two. Amy Brennan, Lucy's daughter, has been a godsend. She's taken them all over the place. They've eaten most of their meals at Morgan's Fire. I've barely seen them."

"I thought you were taking some days off?"

Their hands brushed, and he took hers.

"Maybe next week, or their last week when there's no pony camp. Right now, I'm training a new vegetable chef, or should I say, she's training me. Her name's Cady Peltzer. She's amazing. Her food is some of the best I've ever eaten. We're very lucky to have found her." Meryl paused, looking up at him, her hand on his arm. "I'm sorry, I've been babbling. What I really want to say is, I'm glad to see you."

Joe smiled. "You haven't been babbling at all. I'm glad to see you too."

"Tell me about you. How has your week gone?"

He shrugged. "Up and down. As I get more settled here, it seems as if a few unexpected minefields have cropped up."

"Oh?"

"I told you a little about my former parishioners and their adjusting to my new status."

She nodded, waiting for him to explain further.

"I've been—" He stopped, meeting her gaze. "You know... Let's wait and talk about this later. No need to spoil our day."

She checked the kids' location, then turned back to him. "They're fine. Now, tell me, please."

"I've probably told you that I contemplated leaving the church for a few years. I don't regret leaving. Not at all. What I've come to realize lately, however, is how much of me is still a priest. I don't know how to be otherwise. It's part of every fiber of my being. This realization has been unsettling. In fact, I went to talk with my successor, Father Flynn, this past week. He was very helpful."

"That's good."

"He suggested a retreat might be a way to transition. Quiet time away from here might help me to figure out who I am now."

"That sounds wise."

"So, I've applied to spend time at a retreat center, The Arbors. It's an hour and a half north on the southern coast of Maine. They let me know this morning. I have a place as of Tuesday."

"Wow. How many days is the retreat?"

"A month. I return a week before Murph and Greta's wedding."

Her eyes widened as she stared up at him. "A month? I thought you might say three or four days or a long weekend...but a month?"

He took both her hands. "Meryl, I think you know that I have very strong feelings for you. If you ask me not to go, I'll cancel."

While every part of her screamed *no, no, no*, she said, "Of course, you must go. I'll be here when you get back, and maybe we can keep in touch in some way?"

He shook his head. "They recommend no contact with the outside world. No phones, mail, email, nothing."

Meryl swallowed, her heart aching. "We better catch up with the kids." She let go of his hands and began walking.

"Meryl," he cried as she quickened her pace.

THEY CAUGHT UP WITH THE KIDS IN THE CLEARING THEY'D CHOSEN. Packs had been thrown aside, and Kip and Gigi were climbing the boulders along the cliff.

"Careful up there!" Meryl called as she spread the quilt, then her towel.

Joe set down his load. "Are you okay?"

She gazed up, meeting his eyes. "It was a surprise just as we... Well, what I mean is...just as we were getting closer."

"I know." He wanted to say more, so much more, but in truth, their relationship was part of what he wished to examine from a distance. Had he jumped into a passionate affair too soon after a lifetime of celibacy? He knew he loved Meryl, very deeply, but were his feelings right or even real?

"Let's just enjoy this beautiful day, shall we?"

As he nodded, the kids raced up. "What's for lunch?" Kip asked. Gigi flopped down on the quilt.

Joe opened the pack and took out bags from the Café containing the sandwiches he had ordered and picked up as per Meryl's text earlier in the morning.

"As requested, we've got ham and cheese for you." He handed Kip a large, wrapped panini. "And turkey for Gigi. Help yourself to drinks. I got waters, lemonade, and iced tea. He then handed Meryl her BLT and brought out what looked like the same for himself. "They asked if I wanted to add avocado and I said yes. Is that okay?"

"Perfect." She selected one of the teas and handed it to him, then took another for herself. "Thank you for getting all this, Joe. Kids?"

"Thanks, Joe!" Gigi said. "This is really good."

"Mine too, thanks," Kip echoed.

They spent the meal telling Joe about their week at pony camp, clearly a huge success. They had made new friends, and they loved spending time at the stables and the farm. "The Morgans have the coolest house ever, and their cook is awesome," Kip said. Meryl had heard that most kids were picky eaters, but not these two. They both had sophisticated palates and seemed ready to consume anything they were served.

"The last night of camp, there's a sleepover. They're pitching tents behind the barn and there's gonna be a bonfire. Can we go, Aunt Meryl?" Gigi asked.

"Sounds fun," she said, making a note to discuss the details with Weezie at Monday morning drop-off.

After lunch and several of Meryl's cookies, Gigi and Kip wanted to climb down to the beach to look for "stuff." The water was still frigid, but she suspected it wouldn't stop them from venturing in, hence her insistence that they bring a change of clothes. As the kids ran off, she and Joe cleaned up the lunch things and then headed for the beach path.

Like much of the shoreline, the beach was mostly rocky with occasional patches of sand. It was low tide, and the kids turned over rock after rock, screaming as green crabs scuttered away, hiding in crevices and under the rockweed. Nearer to the water, they found eels and a few sea urchins and a starfish.

"Wish we'd brought a bucket," Gigi said as she dipped her toes into the icy water. "Look, a horseshoe crab! No, two!" she called, pointing.

Meryl and Joe came closer to look, and Kip took hold of one of the crab's tails and lifted it up. "Cool," he said. The crab's body, legs, and claws flexed and fluttered, waiting to be released.

Gigi frowned. "Put him down, Kip. Remember what Tim said at dinner the other night?"

She referred to Tim Miller, Richard's son-in-law who was married to his daughter Gail. Tim was a woodworker and lobster fisherman, but he also helped monitor poachers along the river who caught horseshoe crabs illegally to use for bait.

"I'm not gonna kill him." He set the creature down in the shallow water, and it glided out of sight.

"That was a 'her,'" Joe said. "The big ones are usually females."

Meryl looked at him, and he shrugged. "You're surprised, but don't forget I've lived here most of my life. You pick up a few things. I've also had the pleasure of going out with Tim and some other fishermen from time to time. Those crabs might be my all-time favorite animals."

"Really?" Gigi said. "Why?"

"Well, they've been around since the dinosaurs, so that makes them pretty resilient. Their blood is also used for certain medicines."

"Really?" Gigi said, looking up at him. "Do they have to kill them for that?"

"Nope. That's the cool part. They catch them, withdraw blood, then release them. Horseshoe crabs also help keep the red knot population thriving. Red knots are shorebirds, and the two species have a mutually supportive relationship. One of the red knots' food sources is horseshoe crab eggs."

As the kids waded farther into the water, Meryl said, "That's so interesting."

He nodded. "Someone told me about a documentary concerning the relationship between the crabs and red knots. I think it's called *The Tale of Two Species*. Fascinating."

She moved closer and linked her arm through his. "You are a constant surprise, Joe O'Leary."

He smiled, taking her hand and pulling her closer. "Wouldn't want to be too boring."

She leaned over, resting her head on his shoulder. "Never."

CHAPTER 15

When they returned from the beach, they all tumbled into Joe's truck for the short ride to the docks, where they bought four lobsters off the boat. After a stop at Moon and Stars, they were home again with the makings of a delicious meal. Joe made a salad from whatever he could find in the fridge, and Gigi set the table. Kip professed himself to be an expert lobster cooker and was therefore in charge of that aspect of their dinner. After showering, Meryl set out a charcutier board with cheeses, crackers, some excellent prosciutto, and assorted olives and vegetables. When Joe spied the finished product, he whistled. "This is a whole new level of eating for me."

She laughed. "These are hot right now, so I'm trying to experiment with different combinations."

"Lucky us."

"And we're lucky with our budding gourmands too. I've yet to find anything they won't try. For all her flakiness, I think Sherry moves in fancy circles and drags them along with her."

"They are lucky kids to be here with you."

"Maybe," Meryl said. "Let's wait and see if they survive."

~

MERYL GROANED AS SHE POPPED A BUTTERY MORSEL OF LOBSTER INTO her mouth. "This is incredible, Kip. The lobsters are cooked to perfection. I think we should hire you both at Field and Fire. Gigi sets a perfect table, and our chef could learn a thing or two from you," she added, winking at her nephew.

"She's right," Joe said. "I've had a lot of lobsters over the years, but none this good."

Gigi gazed over at her aunt. "Maybe our last week here since we won't have camp, we can come and help at the restaurant? I've waitressed for my mom at the yacht club."

"Let's think about that," Meryl said, intrigued by Gigi's comment and the realization that she knew next to nothing about her half sister or her life. "What exactly is your mom's job?"

"She the manager of the yacht club," Gigi said.

"Assistant manager," her brother corrected, with an eye roll thrown in for good measure.

"Yeah, but she does all the work. Her lard-ass boss is never there. Sorry for swearing, Joe. Chuckie Potts is not a nice person, and he's lazy as hell. Oops, sorry! I did it again."

"I'm sorry to hear that," Meryl said. "Does he make it hard for your mom, then?"

She shrugged. "Sometimes."

"Hey, Joe, can you pass the bread?" Kip asked. "And can we please change the subject? Last thing we need to be talking about is that slime bag."

After a brief, awkward silence, Meryl asked them about plans for the next day, and the mood lightened. After cleaning up, she suggested walking into town for ice cream at Cove Creamery. They took their cones to the small village green on the south side of Main Street and sat on two of the park's ten stone benches. The backs of each bench held memorial tiles honoring the village's veterans. Kip and Gigi sat together, with Joe and Meryl nearby.

Meryl shivered in the cool of the evening. "We may have rushed the season with these."

Joe slipped his arm around her shoulders. "This has been a wonderful day. Thank you, Meryl."

"Thank you...for joining us and for our picnic."

He took her hand. "I'm sorry if I sprang the retreat on you so abruptly."

"I understand," she said, her voice low. "This is a huge change for you."

"I hope I haven't taken advantage of you and your feelings."

"I'm an adult. I fully participated in all of this," she said, gesturing between them. "Happily, I might add." As she leaned against his shoulder, another involuntary shiver passed through her.

Joe sat up and slipped out of his jacket, draping it around her. "Maybe we should head back."

They called the kids and began the walk home, taking a shortcut behind the green. The path wound around until it eventually opened onto Beach Road. When they reached the cottage, the kids ran in, leaving them in the driveway.

"Coffee?" she asked.

His hands cupped her face. "I'd better not. Early day tomorrow. Any chance you could have dinner with me tomorrow night? I'd love to see you one more time before I go."

"I'm guessing it's to be a sans kids dinner?"

He laughed. "I was hoping, but either way is fine."

"I'll see if Amy is free. Night, Joe," she said, standing on tiptoes to kiss him. A brief friendly kiss.

She stood on the front stoop, waving until he drove off. *A beautiful love affair over before it's begun.*

CHAPTER 16

After dropping the kids at camp, Meryl spent a few hours at Field and Fire doing paperwork. Mondays were always quiet, and she found herself alone for much of the time. Rori stopped by, as did Sandy and Murph, but she saw no one else until she headed out to her car and spied Cady Peltzer strolling along the path from the winery. They had arranged for the thirty-two-year-old vegetable chef to stay temporarily in the manager's apartment, which Wolfie had yet to occupy. Dressed in cut-off jeans, scuffed Doc Martens, and a faded Wu-Tang Clan T-shirt, her spiky red-and-black hair was pulled back in a wide headband. Cady's arms, legs, and neck were covered with tattoos. For health reasons, Sandy had insisted she remove her nose and lip piercings.

"Morning!" Meryl called.

"Hey, boss!" Cady said, her bright gray eyes sparkling with warmth. She had a gorgeous smile, flawless skin, and an ethereal beauty no amount of body art could conceal. "Didn't expect you in."

"Just stopped by. On my way out. How are you settling in?"

"Great. Explored the town with Coco, Sammy, and Wolfie's girlfriend last night," she said, referring to the pantry and sous chefs, and Lyddie.

"Not Wolfie?"

Cady grinned. "Apparently they're not speaking."

"What hot spots did you hit?"

"We ate at Busters, then ended up at Sandy's."

"Oh, what did you think?"

"Veggie burgers sucked."

"Busters is known for their beef burgers. My guess is the veggie versions are frozen."

"That's bullshit. A burger place should know meat or meatless. Their burgers should be fresh and delicious."

"What did you think of Sandy's?"

"Cool. Great band playing. Field and Fire's terrific and all, but why did the boss trade that life for this?"

"I guess he wanted a change. New challenges?"

Cady shrugged. "Whatever floats your boat, I guess."

"Anything I can do for you before I head out?"

"No, thanks. I just thought I'd spend some time when things are quiet. I have a few more recipes I want to try. I did add my food order to the master list."

"Great. As you know, Sandy's invited a bunch of people to come over in the new few weeks. Can't wait to hear their feedback. I'll bet they'll be over the moon."

"Hope so. Enjoy your day."

Shortly after noon, Gigi and Kip called to let her know that they'd be staying at Morgan's Fire for dinner. Meryl double-checked with Amy, then decided to spend the afternoon house cleaning and reading. It felt good to relax, as she allowed herself so little time to herself. As she sat on the porch, gazing out at the river, her cell rang.

"Hey, girl!"

"Johnny?" They'd been texting daily with updates on the kids' stay, but this was the first phone call.

"How's it going?"

"Same as when you texted earlier. I hate to jinx things, but it's been remarkably easy so far and they seem to be having a ball. We'll see next week with no camp. They want to come work at the restaurant."

"Great idea! So how would you feel about one more visitor?"

"Really?"

"I haven't seen you or the kids in ages. Got room for me?"

"Of course. The kids can share, and you can take Kip's room, or there's the Murphy bed in the study."

"Who doesn't love a Murphy bed?"

Me, thought Meryl, who had found most Murphy beds incredibly uncomfortable. "When are you coming?"

"I thought Saturday?"

"Great."

"I know you're working, so I can watch the kids or help at the restaurant. Can't wait to meet the beau too."

"He'll be gone."

"Oh?"

"It's a long story. I'll tell you when you get here. I'm so glad you're coming, brother dear."

"Me too."

They rang off, and Meryl set down her book, then headed upstairs for a quick shower. Joe had texted to suggest that they eat at the Grille in town. She chose a light blue top that swirled with flowers, and black slacks. Both hugged her body, making her feel wanton and sexy, and the blue made her eyes pop, according to Rori, who'd complimented her on the blouse several weeks earlier. She donned silver earrings, a thick hammered silver bangle bracelet, and black flats. Then, after running her fingers through her hair, she headed downstairs, setting a light jacket and her purse by the front door.

Joe arrived just before seven and declined the offer of a drink. As he kissed her lightly on the cheek, he said, "I made reservations for seven, so I'm a bit behind schedule."

The Grille was owned and run by Rosa and Cesar Rodriguez, Sandy's parents. Like Frankie, Rosa was also a Darn Yarner. The lady herself met them at the door. Plump with dark hair, not a hint of gray, her violet eyes were arresting. "Hello, hello, what an honor to have an illustrious chef dining with us."

Meryl hugged her. "The honor is all mine. I love Cesar's cooking."

Their hostess ushered them to a quiet table in the back. "As requested," she said, meeting Joe's eyes as she waved them into their seats. Handing each a menu, she said, "Milania will be over shortly. Can I ask her to bring you something from the bar?" They both ordered the house Chianti, and Rosa disappeared.

Milania, Rosa and Cesar's daughter, soon appeared with their wine. Milania, or Milly, spent her days waitressing at the Café and some nights working for her parents. "Hey, guys, great to see you. Have you decided, or would you like a bit of time?"

"Hi, Milly," Meryl said, smiling at the young woman with dark hair and blue eyes. "I'm going to have the Pesto Bianco."

"Great choice. People have been raving about it tonight. And you?" she said, turning to Joe.

"I'm going to try the Trentino-Alto Adige. It sounds delicious."

"It's my Papa's signature dish. A little spicy. Some people say it's like Hungarian goulash."

"Which I love," he said, grinning as he handed her his menu.

"No appetizers?" Milly asked. When they declined, she nodded. "Okay, then, I'll put this in and bring your salads."

"Thank you, Milly," Meryl said.

When Milly disappeared, Joe set down his wine and reached across the table, taking her hands. "So here we are. How are you holding up, Aunt Meryl?"

"Great. The kids have been happy, and my brother is coming next weekend. I'm excited about that. Kids will be too."

"That's wonderful. I'll be sorry to miss him."

Meryl shrugged. "Someday."

"So, you've survived so far?"

"Amy's been a huge help. They have their pony camp on Friday at the farm. Then Amy's taking them to the water park in Northport Saturday night, after which Richard has invited them to stay at the farm for Sleepover Saturday, a name I suspect he made up for their benefit. He's got a couple of his older grandchildren involved as well."

"He is something, isn't he?"

"Yes, he is. He's worked hard his whole life, been wildly successful, and now lives every day to the fullest."

"How nice that he and Lucy found each other. I like Rob Brennan, her first husband, and he's an excellent physician, but she and Richard seem perfectly suited."

"Are you all packed?"

"Not much to pack, but yes. I'm packed, my clients have been contacted. Andy's secretary kindly sent out letters for me and then followed up with phone calls. She's also booked appointments for a month from now."

"That's optimistic news. You'll be coming back, then."

"Of course, I will. There's the wedding, and there's also my life here. Especially there's you."

"Thank you for saying that."

"It's true."

She squeezed his hands, then withdrew hers and took a sip of wine. "So, tell me about this retreat and how you made this decision."

He laughed. "How far back would you like me to go?"

She regarded him quizzically for a few seconds, then said, "As far as you like. We have all evening."

"I'm not sure I've told you that I'm the oldest of six. My father was a professor of theology. He toyed with the priesthood, but then pursued academia, but never stopped hoping one of his offspring would take to the cloth. As a good Catholic, he became distressed, annoyed, and finally furious at my forays into comparative religions as an undergraduate. I was particularly intrigued with Buddhism and learned transcendental meditation my junior year at Williams."

"They offered a course?"

"At a nearby center, not on campus. When meditating, I felt as if I'd finally come home. The strictures of Catholicism had alarmed me growing up, and I'd had a tempestuous relationship with the church since early adolescence. Much to my father's dismay, my brothers and sisters began exploring other religions as well. There were many possibilities for divergence. That was Lenox and Williamstown in those days. Still is, in a way."

"But as an academic, wouldn't your dad welcome your curiosity and openness?"

"Fine for his students, not his children. During the summer after my junior year, he took me on a four-day road trip, just the two of us. He spent every waking minute expounding upon the importance of a spiritual life and my critical job as a role model for my brothers and sisters. By the end of the trip, I was applying to seminary. I never looked back."

"What a change," she said, nodding as Milly set down their salads.

"My father could be very persuasive. He convinced me that the issues I had with the church were precisely why the priesthood needed me. To be an agent for change and inclusiveness. I believed him. I plunged myself into my studies at seminary with appropriate religious fervor."

"Remarkable."

Joe smiled. "Yes, it was, I suppose."

"So, you liked seminary?"

He grinned. "It was intense, enlightening, and astonishing. I didn't want to leave. In fact, thanks to grants and scholarship funding, I stayed long enough to earn a doctorate, simultaneously completing my deaconship and apprenticeship before graduating. This meant that I went straight from Boston College to St. Mary's. I still wasn't sure the priesthood was for me, but off I went. A few months later, my young parishioner Aislan O'Neill died suddenly, and I knew at once that I'd found my calling."

"Murph's sister?" She'd heard bits and pieces of the tragic, accidental death of her coworker's twin.

"Yes."

"So heartbreaking."

"Supporting Aislan's family during that terrible time, comforting them as they dealt with their loss, has been one of the greatest privileges of my life. I love my family, but the O'Neills are dearer to me than my own flesh and blood."

"I can only imagine," Meryl said, reaching across to touch his hand.

"After that, Catholicism took hold of me, consumed me, really. It's only now, almost thirty years later, that I've began to question again. This could be related to my father's death last year. He was no longer gazing over my shoulder. But, enough about me. Let's enjoy these beautiful salads."

They spent the remainder of the meal chatting about Meryl's childhood, which she pronounced to be somewhat bumpy but unremarkable, and Joe's interest in meditation and most recently the nonsecular meditation, mindfulness, which he often integrated into his counseling practice. When Milly appeared to clear their plates, they were pleasantly sated with food and wine.

"Please tell your parents the meal was divine," Meryl said.

"Mom'll probably check in before you go. She wants to comp you dessert and coffees."

"Oh gee, I'm not sure I could fit dessert," Meryl said, gazing over at Joe.

Milly raised an eyebrow. "You could also split something?"

"What do you recommend?" Joe asked.

"Everyone goes for the tiramisu or cannoli, but I love the panna cotta. It's so light and creamy. You can have it with either chocolate or caramel sauce drizzled over."

"Sounds perfect," Meryl said. "I'll let Joe pick the sauce."

"Why choose? I'll bring both on the side," Milly said. "Sound good?" They both nodded, and she hurried off.

Joe shook his head. "Between Field and Fire and this place, not to mention Bannisters up the coast and all the great seafood joints, I'm surprised every foodie in New England hasn't moved here."

"Oh, they come, believe me. We get people from Maine, Vermont, Connecticut, all over. Even New York."

Rosa Rodriguez appeared. "How was everything?"

"Perfect," Meryl said. "My pesto bianco was sublime."

"And I would have licked my bowl if I dared," Joe said.

"Bellissimo! The Trentino-Alto Adige is my Cesar's specialty. He doesn't make it every night. He'll be so pleased to hear you liked it. And what did you choose for dessert?"

When they told her they'd ordered the panna cotta she insisted they have cappuccino with it. Waving away their protests, she said, "Enjoy!" and scurried off.

Meryl smiled. "I actually meant to order a cappuccino."

"Good," he said.

After oohing and ahhing at each bite of the panna cotta, they sipped their cappuccinos, and Joe asked if she'd like to take a drive along the coast. She agreed, he settled the bill, and they waved goodbye to Rosa, who was sitting at the end of the bar chatting with another woman. Meryl recognized her as another Darn Yarner, Hope Childs, who owned a yoga studio in town. Shortly after her arrival, she'd gone to several Cove Yoga classes, and continually told herself she would go back when things calmed down. *Ha!*

JOE DROVE NORTH ALONG THE COAST ROAD AS FAR AS SANDY'S. THE wide wood-and-steel structure ablaze with lights hung over the cliffs, the ocean crashing below. Rock music blared, reverberating and mingling with the roar of the waves. He turned the truck around in the parking lot and suggested that they drive the short distance to Sebring Park and take a walk along the seawall.

"Are you sure? Don't you have an early start tomorrow?"

"Not too early."

"Okay, then, it might be good to walk off some of my dinner."

A grassy, three-acre park at the edge of the cliffs, Sebring Park was the brainchild of the Darn Yarners. The eight friends had raised funds for its creation almost twenty years earlier. Most recently, they had added a labyrinth, which was illuminated at night, visited and enjoyed by many in the neighboring communities.

Joe and Meryl held hands as they followed the labyrinth's path to its center and back out. They then set out along the dirt path bordering the cliffs. A half mile south, they stopped at a spot where the path led between two huge boulders forming a sort of gateway to the next section of trail. They had passed several couples and bunches of teenagers on the popular walk, but now were alone with no one in sight.

His back against a boulder, Joe pulled her close. "I'll miss you, my sweet, beautiful Meryl." His lips found hers, and she opened herself to him.

After a few seconds, she pulled back. "I'll miss you too."

"We've never talked about your love life. Your past love life, I mean," he said.

She put her hands on his chest and looked up at him, "And you've decided that this is the time to do it?"

He laughed. "I know. Bad timing. What an ass I am. It just popped into my head."

"Well, pop it out again and I'll give you a report when we're bored someday."

They kissed again, but she could sense his resistance, as if he didn't want to take things further. A few minutes later, they turned back, walking hand in hand toward Sebring Park.

Halfway to the car, she said, "Okay, if you really want to know. I had the usual college romances, then a somewhat long-term relationship years ago when my brother and I were running a restaurant in California. That eventually petered out. Romance is difficult if you're in the restaurant business. No time, no energy.

"Then there was Giovanni. I met him in Florence."

"Giovanni?" Joe said, turning to gaze down at her.

"Giovanni De Ganni. I met him when he took a few women and me to a leather coat factory, one of his many sidelines. We subsequently had a brief but passionate affair. I knew he had women up and down the coast, but he was an Adonis, a beautiful Italian Adonis. You know how they talk about lucid dreams?" Joe smiled, nodding. "Giovanni was mine. When I woke up, it was time to come home."

"What about the coat?"

She laughed. "I wore it once."

They had reached the car now, and he opened her door. As she moved by him, he whispered, "I love you, Meryl."

Startled, she paused, meeting his eyes, then reached up, her hand caressing his cheek. "I love you too."

Another dream over? Quiet on the ride home, they kissed on her doorstep, a brief sweet kiss, and then he drove away, taking her heart with him. *Did I learn nothing from Giovanni?* she thought, watching the truck round the bend out of sight. *Only this time, it's not other women, but something else entirely.*

CHAPTER 17

Johnny arrived in a whirlwind Saturday afternoon. Tan and fit, with sandy hair, he kept in shape through careful eating and daily exercise, his favorite, swimming. Two decades separated sister and brother in age, although he looked ten or fifteen years younger than his sixty-two years. Their parents had been in high school when Johnny was born and didn't have Meryl until their late thirties.

The kids said brief hellos and then went off with Amy to the water park.

"Have fun!" Johnny called as they hustled out with towels as well as duffels and sleeping bags for Sleepover Saturday.

"Sounds like twenty-four-seven summer camp around here," he said as they watched Amy drive away.

"It really is," his sister said, patting his shoulder. "So good to have you here. I'll get you over to the farm soon to meet Richard, Lucy, and their families. They're amazing people."

Johnny draped his arm over her shoulder as they headed inside. "And how is this amazing person doing? Clearly, you're Auntie of the Year. How 'bout otherwise?"

Meryl shrugged. "Okay. It's been fun to have the kids here. I'm happy I said yes."

"Why do I sense a 'but' somewhere?"

"Work's been crazy and, of course, there's Joe."

"Tell me all! I want to hear every salacious detail!"

"Ha-ha."

The day was unseasonably warm, with a gentle breeze from the river. They grabbed iced teas, sat on the porch, and Meryl related the saga of the past few weeks. "And now he's gone," she said in conclusion. "And I honestly don't know what will happen when he returns. For all I know, he may have an epiphany during the retreat and decide to return to the priesthood."

"Can you do that?"

"Who knows? Maybe after a brief love affair, he's ready to return to a celibate life."

"Priests do marry in some parts of the world, you know."

"Not in this part." She set down her empty glass and stood to stretch.

They strolled down her dock, watching boats go by. Fish were jumping, and the gulls and cormorants squawked and dove all around them. "Have you got a pole?" he asked. "I can catch our dinner."

"Your dinner? Sorry, big brother. There's plenty of food here, but I have to be at Field and Fire in an hour."

"Then I'm coming. You can put me to work."

Meryl started to protest, but then stopped. She loved working with her brother and knew no matter what she asked him to do, he'd fall into a rhythm within minutes. She also knew her coworkers would enjoy him. "Chef de Tournant, it is. We can always use a swing cook, and Coco, our pantry chef, always needs help. That's usually me, so you and I will be side by side again."

"Good girl!" he said, grabbing a crab net and scooping up a large blue crab. "Appetizer?"

She laughed. "No, thank you, but knock yourself out."

∾

"Your brother's a hoot," Rori said as she passed through the kitchen with a stack of menus.

"Yes, he is," Meryl said. "And since he and Coco have things under control, I'm going to do the rounds and say hi to people. Be great to get feedback on Cady's selections."

"You mean you're not sending tattoo woman out to schmooze?"

Meryl gave her a look. "I could, and she'd be terrific. But she's kind of busy. People have been ordering the new entrées all night."

As she made the rounds, the accolades continued, with everyone raving about Cady's dishes. One of Meryl's last stops was to say hello to Jack and Lolly Faulkner. The newlyweds sat at a table by the window and were dining with Richard and Lucy. In addition to their business partnership, the two women were best friends.

"How's it going?" she asked, gazing around the table. She liked both couples and envied them their friendship. Both men were gorgeous, Richard craggy, lean, and tall, Jack broad-shouldered and stockier, and their wives both beautiful. Like her husband, Lucy was slender and tall. All curves, Lolly had arresting violet eyes and thick, dark hair that fell around her shoulders and down her back.

"Best meal I've had in years," Lolly said. "And we're surrounded by unbelievable chefs between here, my mother's place, and the Grille. Don't tell anyone I said that, though. We even got our meat-and-potatoes husbands to go vegetarian tonight."

"Not vegan," Jack said. "Not ready to go that far. I have to admit, my mushroom Wellington was fantastic."

"As was my Aussie meatless pie," Richard said. "Although on a cold winter night, I could never give up Callie's Guinness beef pie."

Lucy laughed, winking at Meryl. "That's the beauty of it, isn't it? You can have both. Please tell your chef that my cauliflower gratin with manchego and almond sauce was sublime. Where did she find the manchego?"

"We have a cheese supplier in New York. We like to use local for most everything, including the cheeses, but sometimes we have to import. We have a local artisan cheese company that makes a variety of goats milk cheeses. They've committed to making a Manchego-like cheese for us, but the aging process is sixty days to two years."

"No wonder it's so delicious," Lucy said.

"Who's the local supplier?" Richard asked.

"We have a couple, actually. We buy almost anything the O'Neills will save for us. They have goats and are willing to experiment, but the main supplier will be Coastal Creamery. They're a much bigger operation."

"Hmm... I wonder how long it would take us to gear up for cheese production. We could get the cow's milk, start buying more goats, build another barn, hire cheesemakers, and—"

"Here we go!" Lucy said.

"I'm loving this idea," her husband said. "We sold our goat milk in Maine. You know how I love goats. Jack, maybe you'd like to get in on this?"

Meryl grinned. Richard Morgan was legendary in his development of successful businesses. Once he set his mind on something, it usually took off. She couldn't tell if it was the wine and a good meal talking, but she wouldn't have been at all surprised to learn that Morgan's Fire Cheese Company would be in operation soon. "Well, I'll leave you to your dreams. I hope you're having dessert."

"Already ordered," Jack said. "I can always find room for your berry tart."

"Good choice," Meryl said, nodding as she moved to say hello to one more table before heading back to the kitchen. As she passed Sandy in the bar, her boss grinned, the smile that had sent many a woman into a swoon.

"Cady's food is a hit," she said.

"Sure is. Thanks, Meryl." After giving her a thumbs-up, he joined Murph behind the bar.

At the end of the night, restaurant now empty, some of the staff sat around in the darkened dining room, enjoying a drink or glass of wine. Sandy and Murph had gone home, but Rori and most of the kitchen staff were gathered near the fireplace, chatting and laughing, mostly at Johnny's anecdotes collected over a lifetime spent in kitchens all over the world. Finally, Meryl stood and said, "Come on, brother dear. You can come back any night this week, but I'm beat."

"Nice crew," he said as they drove home. "Talented too."

"I'm lucky."

"Almost makes me want to relocate and come out of retirement."

"Really?"

"I said 'almost.' I'm not masochistic. I love retirement, especially because I get to be with my campers out west every summer."

"Some year I'd love to come out there and spend a few days."

"It's an extraordinary place. The Morgans are superheroes. Both the East Coasters and the Westerners."

"Sure seems so."

As they turned onto Beach Road, he asked, "So what's the plan for tomorrow?"

"There isn't one. I thought I'd ask the kids. There was some talk of riding. You game?"

"On a horse?"

"Yes."

"Better be a slow one."

"We'll see." As she pulled into the driveway, she thought about Joe and how far away he seemed. She wondered if she'd ever feel his strong arms around her again, making her feel warm, safe, and loved.

CHAPTER 18

Joe settled into an easy rhythm at the Arbors. The spartan but comfortable accommodations suited his needs. Each one-room cabin had a tiny kitchen, bathroom, queen-size bed and a sitting area with a small sofa and chairs. A porch ran along the front, with two rocking chairs enabling one to sit and enjoy the ocean view. A short walk across open fields led to paths down to the rocky shore. All twenty cabins appeared similarly outfitted, the distance between each allowing for quiet and privacy. While they were discouraged to do so, guests were allowed to bring laptops, although there was no Wi-Fi service. Residents were encouraged to leave their phones with the front desk, which Joe did when he checked in. The only television was in the main building.

He had brought lots of reading materials and intended to write as well. His first days proved to be singularly unproductive as he could think of nothing but Meryl, her scent, her touch, her kisses, her soft skin, her beautiful eyes gazing into his. Eyes that saw straight into his soul. He loved everything about her. He was sure of it, yet the thought was unsettling, as if he was going against a lifetime of beliefs and commitments. Finally, realizing that his lack of concentration meant he could neither read nor write, he took to taking long walks in the morning and afternoon, losing himself in the beauty of the surrounding countryside.

Nature had always provided solace for him. As the days went on and the weather remained beautiful, he gave himself over to the sights and sounds of the outdoors, to the rich scent of pine and salty breezes, to the feel of the wind on his cheeks as he spent long hours hiking along the beach, gamboling over rocks and boulders like a mountain goat.

He took his meals in the main building. Breakfast was silent, and he enjoyed the quiet after a daily ninety-minute yoga and meditation class. Lunch and dinner he ate alone or with small groups of people who wandered in and out. After the first few days, his frequent meal companions became George, a teacher who was staying in the northernmost cabin, and Lilibet, Joe's nearest neighbor, in the cabin to the south of his. The center encouraged residents to wear name tags, which were always available on a table outside the dining room. Lilibet's plastic-covered tag featured a bold cursive signature surrounded by garlands of flowers. Joe complimented her on it their first lunch together, and she beamed.

"What would you expect from an artiste?" George said, bowing slightly and waving his hand at her.

Both George and Lilibet were older than him. Joe guessed them to be in their early sixties. As the days went by, the three sought each other out both at meals and the occasional walk. Joe looked forward to seeing George and Lilibet and felt a pang of disappointment when they were otherwise engaged. As a single person, he'd always treasured shared meals. While he'd accepted solitary meals as a part of his life, he never liked them. Most times when at home, he'd eat while reading, or in the evenings, while watching television. For his decades as St. Mary's priest, he received frequent dinner invitations from parishioners, and took most Sunday dinners with the O'Neills, but when he left the priesthood, invitations mostly vanished.

Joe had discussed with Fiona and Murphy Senior what to do about Sundays, and they agreed that they should reach out to Father Flynn and invite him on another day, but still dine with Joe on

Sundays. He'd tried to protest as he knew that two dinners would be difficult for Fiona, who worked from dawn to dusk every day, but the couple shooed away his objections, saying that Murph would take up the slack. "We can also ask Greta and Murphy Junior to bring dishes on Sundays," she'd added. "No worries."

No worries indeed, Joe had thought, but also knew further protests were in vain.

≈

"GIVE ME A NAG," JOHNNY SAID. "THAT'S WHAT I WANT, YOUR OLDEST, slowest nag."

He, Meryl, and the kids stood outside Morgan's Run Stables Sunday afternoon with Weezie Morgan and her brother Rich's fiancée, Karen Miller. Karen's family owned Land's End, the huge farm that stretched for miles to the Point. Karen was an experienced rider and had volunteered to come along. She'd also recruited her best friend, Harriet, wife of Kyle Morgan, nephew of Richard and the village veterinarian.

The friends were a study in contrasts. Karen was short, compact, and strong, with curly brown hair and intense lapis-blue eyes. Harriet was taller, slender, with long straight brown hair and soft green eyes. They had ridden from Land's End with four of their horses.

Weezie gave Johnny a look. "Unfortunately, we don't have any nags, per se, but Crackers here is very gentle." She indicated one of their most reliable stable horses, an American Paint already saddled and ready to go.

"Okay, I'm gonna trust you, doll. Don't let me down," Johnny said, approaching the horse, who nudged his hand as he reached up to pet her muzzle.

All found horses and mounted, leaving one horse, Patrick, a stable horse, saddled with no rider. Weezie pulled out her cell and made a call. "Dad, we're all set. Are you coming or not? Patrick's ready to go. Fine, okay. He's tied up. We not going on the Loop. We're heading north to the old bridle path." She clicked off and tucked the phone in her back pocket, turning to the group. "My dad's coming, but he says he'll catch up with us. Probably kill himself doing it. Come on."

"Why don't we give him five minutes?" Meryl suggested. "We truly aren't in a hurry."

"Five minutes, then," Weezie said, settling down on Piccolo, a gentled brown mustang with a white star on his forehead. The horse tossed its head, snorting. "I know, Picci. We'll be going soon."

Two minutes later, Richard appeared in riding boots and a worn black Stetson. "Sorry, folks!" he called as he jogged over to the fence, untied Patrick, and mounted the horse in one fluid motion. He then tipped his hat at his daughter. "Ready, baby. Couldn't miss out on a ride on a day like this, could I?"

Weezie rolled her eyes then took the lead. The others followed, climbing the rise past her mother's bench, then along a trail bordering the cliffs toward Field and Fire and the winery. Despite all his complaining, Johnny sat comfortably in the saddle, riding behind Meryl and the kids. Richard came next, and Harriet and Karen brought up the rear.

"Wow!" Gigi said as she gazed down at the river. "This is awesome."

Weezie looked over her shoulder. "I thought you might like a change from the Loop. We don't bring pony campers this way."

As they crossed the winery property, Wolfie came out to say hi. "Hey, guys. Wish I could come out with you."

"Like you could keep up," his sister said. "How's it going?"

"Busy."

"Have you met everyone?" she asked, waving behind her. "Meryl's niece and nephew—Gigi and Kip, and her brother Johnny?"

Wolfie said hello to the kids, then approached Crackers, petting her nose. "Hey, Johnny, great to see you." He'd met Meryl's brother on a trip to his uncle's in Arizona while researching the wine business. He stayed with Ben and Leonora and consulted with their neighbors who owned Saguaro Vineyards. Then, in his spare time, he'd helped out at Emma's Dream, the camp at the ranch where Johnny served as cook each summer.

Johnny leaned over, nearly slipping off Crackers. "The Wolfman! Great to see you. I've heard amazing things about your work here."

"Mostly due to our vintner Zeke and his assistant. I'm just the front man and party planner. You'll have to come for a tour."

"And he will," Weezie said. "But right now, we're on a ride." She gazed down the drive and spied a car approaching. "And if I'm not mistaken, you've got a visitor!"

Lyddie parked her PT Cruiser in the shade and hopped out. Ignoring Wolfie, she came to say hi to the riders, all of whom she knew. Weezie observed the snub of her brother and gave him a look. "Okay, everyone," she said after several minutes. "Gotta keep going. See ya, Lyddie, brother."

As they rode off, Meryl noticed a scowl on Lyddie's face and assumed they hadn't yet worked out their difficulties. Johnny came up alongside her. "They make a cute couple, but it looks like someone's in trouble."

Meryl shrugged. "Who knows?"

After a leisurely forty-five minute ride, they reached the edge of the Morgan's Fire property and turned west to take the bridle path that ran almost to the main road. Established decades earlier by the previous owners of the vast farm, the wide-open, grassy path was lined with mature white dogwood trees in full bloom. Fallen blossoms blanketed the ground as they proceeded.

"It's like fairy land!" Gigi cried, nudging Sheba forward to ride alongside Weezie and Piccolo.

"Careful," Weezie said. "Picci's still a bit skittish with the stable horses when they get too close."

No sooner had she spoken than her horse reared slightly, then leaned over and nipped the chestnut Morgan. Sheba whinnied and bucked slightly, just enough to throw Gigi to the side of the saddle. With a shriek, she slid off onto the ground.

"Oh Lord," Karen said, nudging Brandi, her brown Arabian,

forward and jumping off to assist Gigi. "You okay?" she asked, grabbing Sheba's reins.

Meryl dismounted and came to her niece's side, holding out her hand. Gigi grabbed it and stood, brushing off, her jeans, now streaked with grass stains. "I'm good. Just wasn't paying attention. Sorry, Weezie."

"No problem. You want to take a few minutes?"

"No, I'm good."

Karen helped her back in the saddle, then whistled to Brandi, wandering at the edge of the path near the woods. When the horse drew up beside her, she mounted, then reined him in, allowing the others to pass. When Harriet came up beside her, Karen clicked, and Brandi fell in beside Rebel, her stable mate. She leaned toward her friend and whispered, "That horse of Weezie's isn't ready for this."

Harriet smiled, and Richard, who rode right behind them, whispered, "Have you ever tried to tell my youngest daughter anything?"

Karen grinned. "It's tricky."

The bridle path ended a mile later, and they turned south, taking advantage of open fields to let the horses go. As most of them galloped across the meadows, Harriet stayed back with Johnny, who preferred a slow canter. When they finally rejoined the others, they found themselves at the north end of a fenced-in yard, a beautiful new farmhouse at its center, the backyard dotted with play equipment—a swing set, seesaw, sandbox, and tiny shingled playhouse that matched the big house.

"What a beautiful property," Meryl said. "Is this the Casey's?"

"Sure is," Richard said, riding up beside her. "Didn't they do a great job? Beautiful house and terrific spot for the kids. Gus and Dennis, his assistant, built the playhouse. Wolfie helped them."

"It's terrific," Meryl said.

"Lucky kids. We sure never had anything like this," Kip said as he gazed around.

Meryl exchanged looks with her brother, and Johnny made a face. From what they'd heard, Sherry moved constantly.

Noticing the siblings' expressions, Richard said, "You've given them lots of memories these past weeks."

"You too," she said. "You, Weezie, and Amy have been so generous and kind to them. I don't know what I would have done without you."

"It's been our pleasure. Lucy and I love having them around. She'd have come today, but she goes to visit her mother on Sundays."

"Well, they won't forget this," Johnny said. "What a spectacular community this is."

Richard nodded. "It's pretty great. My kids and I have lived all over the world. We loved our years in Maine too, but Horseshoe Crab Cove is something else. You'll have to get Kip and Gigi back again. We'd be happy to have them at the farmhouse. We've got lots of room."

"Thanks, Richard," she said as Weezie asked for the group's attention.

"We'll be at the west end of the Loop soon," she called. "Then we'll follow along the north edge before heading back to the stables. Everybody okay? Anyone need a break?"

As they neared the barns, Harriet and Meryl rode side by side. Meryl didn't know Lucy's sister well, but she liked her. Quiet and self-contained, she'd always been warm and welcoming whenever they met. "How are you settling into village life?" she asked.

"I love it. First home I've had in many years."

"And the restaurant's a huge success. You must be thrilled."

"All Sandy's vision."

"And your cooking. Kyle and I are planning to come soon to try the new menu."

"Please do. Cady's food is out of this world."

"I hear you and Joe have been dating a bit."

Meryl blanched.

"Oh, I'm sorry... I've overstepped. I didn't mean to pry."

Shaking herself, Meryl replied, "No, it's fine. Yes, we've been seeing each other for a short while, but he's away now for a month on retreat. Not sure where we stand."

"Oh, I'm sorry."

"It's okay. I'm not sure what will happen, but he's a nice man and has been kind to me and the kids."

"I don't know him well, but that's definitely my impression of him. I know Kyle likes him."

Her heart in her throat, Meryl was relieved when they turned down the drive to the stables and Johnny rode up beside her. "I'm not going to be able to walk when I get off this horse," he said, "so be prepared to carry me."

Meryl laughed. "That's what your niece and nephew are for."

Back at the barn, Harriet and Karen said their goodbyes, declining Richard's offer of drinks at the house and heading back onto to the Loop Trail with the Snowflake and Raven trotting along behind them. Dennis and Gus came out to help with farm horses, and Gigi and Kip volunteered to help brush them down. Richard, Meryl, and Johnny strolled up to the farmhouse, Johnny moaning and groaning the entire way. "What I wouldn't give for a hot tub now," he said as they settled on the porch for a drink.

"Pam and Sandy have one at their place, or there's also Mavis's place. The spa has a great whirlpool," Richard said. Mavis LaSalle, Lolly's mother, owned an elite event property at the east edge of town, complete with mansion, cottages, and spa. "I could call over and get you soaking within the hour."

Johnny waved his hand, laughing. "Oh, don't mind me. I just like to complain. A drink and some ibuprofen before bed will set me right."

"Well, you'll all stay to dinner, then. Callie's making lamb. I know we've got you two master chefs here, but she does a pretty good job with lamb."

"That's too much after our very special afternoon," Meryl protested.

"Nonsense. Lucy's eating at Helen's, Wolfie's out with his girl, so it's just Weezie, Callie, and me. We'd love to have you."

~

SEVERAL HOURS LATER, THE FOUR OF THEM PILED INTO MERYL'S LITTLE car, sated after a delicious dinner of lamb, new potatoes, and green beans topped off with floating island for dessert. Both kids proclaimed the light custardy treat to be the best dessert they'd ever tasted. Their aunt and uncle agreed

"This was an awesome day," Kip said as they drove home.

"Sure was," his sister echoed.

"I'm glad," Meryl said, smiling. "It was awesome, wasn't it? How will we ever top it tomorrow?"

"We've made plans, didn't we tell you?" Kip said.

"Oh?" Meryl said, exchanging glances with Johnny.

"Yeah, a bunch of the kids invited us to hang out. At Rusty Corcoran's house. He lives in town, just off Main Street."

"Was he a camper?" she asked, unable to place the name.

"Yup and his sister Nora was too," Gigi said. "They're cool."

"Well, I guess it'd be okay," she said. "Your uncle and I will find something to do."

"Like lie on the porch and soak in the sun?" he said, eyes half shut.

Later, as she closed her eyes in bed, Meryl's thoughts turned to Joe, and she wondered what he was doing. The pang in her chest subsided after she took deep breaths and eventually fell asleep.

CHAPTER 19

Monday morning, the kids rode to the Corcorans on bicycles they'd borrowed from Morgan's Fire. Meryl and Johnny decided to relax around the house and maybe take a walk after lunch. As she passed through the living room with her watering can to tend to her plants, her brother dressed in one of his wild floral shirts and baggy khakis, raised his head from the sofa and regarded her. "Call him."

"No phones."

"What?"

"I think he either didn't bring his phone or turned it in when he arrived."

"That's a bit extreme."

"It's a retreat. From life, from one's day-to-day routines, and people."

"Surely not twenty-four-seven?"

Meryl shrugged. "Change of subject, please."

"You love him, don't you?"

"What did I just say?"

"Just answer my question and we can talk about anything you like."

"Yes, I love him. I'm crazy about him. Satisfied?"

"No, because people in love stay connected." Johnny was now sitting up, legs crossed, gazing at her with a frown on his face. "This isn't normal."

"Maybe it is for someone who's spent his life as a celibate priest only to jump into a passionate sexual relationship as soon as he walks away from his spiritual home."

"It's been six months."

"Five." Suddenly tired, Meryl flopped on a nearby upholstered chair. "Can we drop this? I know you're trying to help, but the only way I can handle this is to put him out of my mind."

"Like you've been successful with that so far."

"Johnny!"

"Okay, okay. Let's do something. How about a picnic on the beach? I'll make everything."

"Maybe just eat here, then take a walk?"

"That works for me," he said, hopping up. "I'll whip us up something."

"Thanks," she said, reaching out to pat his leg as he passed by.

"What brings you here to The Arbors, Joseph?" Lilibet asked at their second lunch together.

He chuckled. "It's a long, winding tale."

"I'm here for six months, so I have plenty of time, and I'm a good listener."

"And you?"

"My story is short. I lost my husband a year ago, and my kids swooped in to manage me. Apparently, they see it as their job as I approach seventy. I needed to get away, to get reacquainted with me and who I am now, without Phillip."

Joe smiled, passing her a tray of sandwiches that had just been set beside him. "Same as the queen and Prince Phillip. Is that where your name originated?"

"I am Elizabeth, and my parents were both Anglophiles, but the shortened Lilibet came from my younger sister's mispronunciation. Now, back to your long, winding tale."

"Actually, it's not unlike yours. Finding out who I am after a major life change."

When George joined them at dinner, Joe and Lilibet were still discussing his story. He gave their new friend a brief recap. When he finished, George whistled. "That must've been tough for you and your flock. I'm a lapsed Catholic myself. Came here for the meditation. Love the classes here and the simplicity of life."

"So, what's next for you, Joe?" she asked, soft gray-blue eyes regarding him.

"That's what I'm here to find out."

"And what about Meryl?"

"I've confused her, which makes me angry at myself. I took advantage of her when I knew how unsettled I was."

Lilibet set down her ham and cheese sandwich and gave him a look. "Does she see it as taking advantage of her, do you think?"

"No."

"Wish I could be helpful," George said, "but as a lifelong bachelor, I'm out of my depth here."

"Never found the right woman?" Joe asked, looking over at his lunch companion, a handsome sixty-something man with a full head of salt-and-pepper hair, chocolate-brown eyes, and ruddy complexion. Strong and robust, George looked like a man who had spent his life at a physically demanding job, so when he'd told them he'd been a longshoreman for most of his life, Joe wasn't surprised.

"Oh, I'd find 'em from time to time, but truth is, I'm scared of women. They're so mysterious and inscrutable. Never know the right thing to say."

Lilibet laughed. "Well, it's never too late. We could practice while you're here. I forgot to ask yesterday when we met, how long will you be staying?"

"Just a few more weeks, I'm afraid."

She clapped her hands together. "Then we better get cracking! We have lots to do!"

After a lazy lunch of chicken salad on warm baguettes with Johnny's crispy chopped salad on the side, brother and sister grabbed shoes and sweatshirts and prepared for a walk. "How energetic are you feeling?" she asked.

"Pretty good after our lunch."

"We could walk up through town, then along East Road. There's a great walking path at the edge of Mavis Lasalle's property that will take us down to a long stretch of beach. I'm pretty sure it's low tide, so we can walk for miles. Or...if we want to visit that beach, we can park in town and cut a mile or so off the walk."

"Sounds better," he said. "After all, I'm an old man."

"Baloney. Now, come on!" She grabbed her bag, car keys, and a light jacket, then motioned for him to follow. "Bring your windbreaker in case the wind picks up along the shore."

Meryl parked near the community garden and brother and sister walked the short distance to the entrance to Cove Inn and Spa. Through the trees the wide slate rooftop of a stone mansion with twenty chimneys was visible.

"Wow! Quite a place," he said.

"That's the inn, Netherfield Manor," Meryl said. "It's pretty spectacular."

"Is the owner a Jane Austen fan?" he asked, squinting in the sunlight as they gazed at the huge structure.

"Yup. There are a bunch of other buildings, a spa, indoor pool, three cottages, and more. It's a big property. Mavis is Lolly's mom. You met them at the restaurant, remember?"

"Gorgeous long dark hair, violet eyes?"

"Yes. Her mother has those eyes too, but she's thin as a rail and looks more like Morticia from the Addams family."

"Hmm."

"Like her fellow Darn Yarners, Mavis has a good heart and has been very generous to the village. In fact, she donated the land for Laura's Community Garden."

"Don't 'spose she'd give us a tour of her manse, would she?"

"I can call and ask. The inn has an incredible chef, Kendall Reese. You'd enjoy meeting her. Come on, we're going this way." She led him twenty yards beyond the driveway to a path leading into the woods. "This is the beach path. It's on Mavis's land, but all are welcome to use it."

As they followed the half-mile trail along the cliffs through the brush and open fields, they passed by the lawns of shingled guest cottages, then headed down a steep path to the beach. Johnny oohed and ahhed the whole way, already making plans to return and rent one of the cottages.

"Better save your pennies and reserve one now," Meryl said. "They're usually booked two years in advance."

As it was low tide, they found a wide stretch of open beach. They tossed their sneakers on boulders and strolled down to the water's edge. The water was chilly, but they waded in and out, occasionally spotting a blue crab or school of minnows in the clear, calm river. They had walked for twenty minutes northward and were contemplating reversing course when a horse and rider appeared in the distance.

"Wow, now that would be cool," he said. "Why didn't we ride on the beach?"

"Probably because it's a bit trickier to get down here. That's Weezie. Is she alone?"

"Looks like it," Johnny said, shielding his eyes as they paused to watch her draw closer.

"Hi, guys!" Weezie called, waving as she approached, reining in Piccolo when she reached them. "Perfect day, huh?"

"Couldn't be better," Johnny said.

"Where are the kiddos?"

"They went to their friends' house. The Corcorans? They met at pony camp."

Weezie frowned, sliding off her horse to stand beside them. "Oh? What were they planning?"

"I don't know," Meryl said. "You frowned. Do you see a problem?"

"I like Rusty and Nora, but their older siblings, not so much. I also happen to know that the parents, Mark and Sue are out of town. They do this all the time and leave the older ones in charge. Markie's seventeen and Leonie is sixteen."

"What kind of trouble can they get into here in Mayberry?" Johnny asked.

Weezie rolled her eyes. "You'd be surprised. Hey, don't mind me. I'm sure Gigi and Kip are fine. Maybe when you get back, you can check on them? I'm only basing my opinions on Amy's reports. The Corcorans hired her to stay one weekend, and she said never again. In fact, they called her the other day, which is how I knew Sue and Mark were away."

Meryl and Johnny exchanged looks. "I wish I'd brought my cell phone," she said.

"Here, use mine," Weezie said, pulling it from her pocket and handing it to Meryl.

"I wouldn't know who to call. I haven't memorized the kids' cell numbers."

"I have," her brother said, holding out his hand. He had always had an uncanny recall of number sequences. He put the phone on speaker and punched in numbers. Soon they were listening to Kip's voice message. "Kip call me," he said and punched off, dialing another number.

"Hello?" Gigi's voice. She sounded frightened.

"Hey, Gi, it's Johnny. I'm using Weezie's phone 'cause we're on the beach and our phones are in the car. We're just checking to see how you're doing. Having fun?"

"No," she whispered. "Can you come get me?"

Johnny looked at his companions. "Course we can. Where are you? At the Corcorans?"

"We're at the beach on the other side of that big inn, you know?"

"Barnum's Ledge," Weezie said.

"Are you okay?" he asked.

"Sort of... I fell and hurt my arm, but it's Kip. He's real sick. Throwing up."

"Jeez," Johnny said. "Well, sit tight. We'll be there as soon as we can. Call this number if anything changes, baby."

"We're such a long way from the car. Is there a short cut?"

"Straight up, behind Netherfield," Weezie said., "I'm going to call the inn, see if Jack or someone else can go down. I'll also call my dad. He may be able to get someone there sooner than we can. I'll head back to the farm now. Are you okay finding your way?"

"We'll have to be, won't we?" Meryl said, already scrambling up toward the cliff path.

"You can stop at Netherfield and see if Kendall or Mavis are around. I'm sure they'd drive you to your car," Weezie said, then reined Piccolo around and headed down the beach.

"Our shoes, sis?"

"No time!" she cried, her stomach in knots. Pam Morgan Rodriguez had been talking about the problems with drugs, even with middle schoolers. All she could think about was Pam's mention of oxycodone.

CHAPTER 20

There's no reason I can't call her, Joe thought as he headed up to the main building for an afternoon meditation class. He had time before a special class being offered by a visiting teacher, so he headed to the front desk and asked for his lockbox where residents stored personal belongings.

He carried the box to the back porch of the building. Once settled in a rocking chair, he pulled out his cell phone and turned it on. A minute later, he punched Meryl's number in and waited. She answered on the fourth ring, sounding breathless. "Meryl? It's me. Have I caught you at a bad time?"

"Kind of," she said. "Johnny and I are headed to Barnum's Ledge. Something's happened to the kids. Can I call you back?"

"Of course," he said, as the phone clicked off. *The kids...* She sounded scared to death. He closed the lockbox, retaining the phone and its charger. He wondered if he should drive home, but then decided to wait to hear from her. She had Johnny and many friends in the village. *She doesn't need confused, self-absorbed me.* He turned the phone off and slipped it into his backpack, returning the lockbox to the front desk. After meditation, he would keep the phone with him until he heard from her.

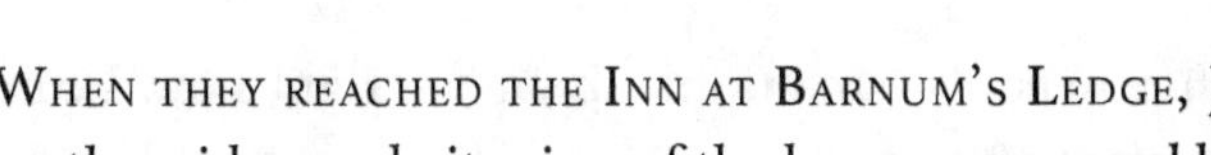

WHEN THEY REACHED THE INN AT BARNUM'S LEDGE, JACK WAS WAITING on the wide porch, its view of the bay unsurpassed by any in the area. "Hey, guys, they're on their way to St. Elizabeth's in Bayport. It's a first-class hospital."

"What happened?" Meryl asked, her eyes wild with fright.

"Looks like your niece may have broken her wrist and the boy's taken something. The EMTs were working on him. The rest of the kids disappeared, but we've got people looking for them."

"Are the kids alone in the ambulance, then?" she said.

"Weezie's with them and Richard followed in the car. The Morgan brothers and Sandy and Tim are looking for the Corcorans and the gang to find out what he took. They'll find them. Would you like me to drive you to Bayport?"

"Thanks, but I know the way," she said. "I've been there a couple of times for appointments."

"Can I get you anything before you leave?"

"Don't suppose you've got two bottles of water handy?" Johnny asked.

"You bet. I'll be right back."

"Oh, Johnny, how could this have happened?" she said, tears streaming down her face.

"They're gonna be fine," he said, folding her into his arms.

Jack returned with their waters, and they took off for the twenty-minute drive to St. Elizabeth's Hospital. "Do you think we should call Sherry?" she asked, realizing that the kids and she had received only one phone call over the past three weeks.

"Let's wait till we get to the hospital, so we'll have an accurate report."

"That's probably best."

Meryl's hands held the steering wheel in a vise grip, knuckles white. He gazed over at her, then said, "What did Joe have to say?"

"Joe? Oh, nothing. I didn't let him before I hung up."

"I heard you tell him the kids were in trouble. He must be worried sick."

Meryl shook her head. "I can't think about Joe right now. I care about him, but he left me."

"To figure things out."

"Can we please not talk about Joe right now?" she said as she pulled into the hospital parking lot.

AFTER WRANGLING WITH THE HOSPITAL STAFF OVER PERMISSION TO treat, a nurse ushered them back to where Gigi lay in a cubicle, her arm in a splint, a PA ministering to her. "She's just back from X-ray," the PA said. "I'm Megan. The attending will be in to see you shortly."

No sooner had they exchanged greetings than a petite thirtysomething in sky-blue scrubs appeared, her thick curly brown hair pulled back in a ponytail, glasses perched on the end of her nose. "Hello, I'm Dr. Mendes, the orthopedist on call."

"We're her aunt and uncle," Meryl said. "Gigi and her brother are staying with me, and we haven't been able to reach her mother."

"That's what I understand from Ms. Morgan, who brought them in. They're treating Kip for a drug overdose upstairs."

Meryl clapped her hand over her mouth. "Oh my God, do they know what he took?"

"He's still unconscious, and his sister doesn't know what he took, or if she does, she's not telling," she said, turning to Gigi, who looked white as a sheet.

"I don't! I wasn't even with them when it happened."

Meryl went to the bedside and placed her arm around Gigi's shoulders, her thin body trembling. "We've got people scouring the village," she told the doctor. "Looking for the others to find out what happened. What about Gigi? What did the X-ray show?"

"She has a broken wrist. I'll cast it, and you can take her home. You're welcome to stay. It won't take long."

Meryl looked at Johnny. "I'd like to check on Kip, or you could?"

"Go," he replied. "I'll stay here with my girl."

Dr. Mendes nodded. "They're probably busy working on him, but take the elevator to the first floor and follow the blue line to the trauma center. There'll be signs along the way."

Meryl hugged Gigi, then her brother, before hurrying down the hall to the bank of elevators. Dr. Mendes was right, there was no one to speak to her in the trauma center, and she was directed to a small waiting room. She pulled out her phone and tried Sherry again. Straight to voicemail. She then dialed Richard Morgan. After asking about the kids, he told her his son-in-law Tim and Wolfie had spotted two of the boys on electric bikes and were giving chase. "They're on the Loop Trail, and I have Gus and Dennis blocking it at this end. We'll grab them soon and be in touch. Hang in there, sweetheart."

Meryl held the phone, wondering if she should call Joe, but then slipped it back in her pocket, her heart heavy and aching. What could he do from Maine? She leaned back and closed her tear-rimmed eyes.

Forty-five minutes later, he walked in the door.

CHAPTER 21

"How did you...? Why are you...? What's happened?"

In answer, he came forward and enveloped her in his strong arms. "I'll explain about me later. How are you?"

At that moment, her phone buzzed. The call ID showed Richard Morgan.

"Hello?"

"We caught up with them. It was oxycodone. Rusty Corcoran got a hold of some pills from his uncle, who takes them for pain. They crushed some and slipped them into Kip's soda without telling him."

"Thanks, Richard," she said, jumping up and turning to Joe. "I've got to let the doctors know."

"I'll come with you."

They hurried down the hall to the nurses' station and found no one behind the desk. "Hello!" Meryl called.

A tall, slender man in green scrubs appeared from the opposite hallway. "Are you the family of Kip Stockdale?"

"Yes, I'm his aunt. His mother is out of the country and unreachable."

"I'm Dr. Farrow. I'm not sure if anyone's updated you?" She shook her head. "Well, your nephew ingested oxycodone."

Meryl nodded. "Yes, we just learned that from the boys he was with."

Farrow continued. "Appears to have been a small amount, probably crushed pills taken orally in a drink. The EMTs administered Narcan immediately, which saved his life and probably prevented any permanent damage. Time will tell. He's resting, but slowly regaining consciousness. We'd like to watch him for an hour or two, get some fluids into him, but then you can take him home."

"Oh, thank God," she said, turning to Joe.

He folded her into his arms and kissed the top of her head. "Can she see him?"

"Nurses are cleaning him up. Quite a bit of vomiting. You didn't happen to bring clean clothes, did you?"

Meryl shook her head.

"I'll go get some, or my bag's in the truck? They'd be baggy, but he could wear something of mine home."

"That would be great. Would you wait and come in with me before you go for the clothes?"

"Of course."

KIP APPEARED TO BE SLEEPING WHEN THEY STEPPED INTO THE ROOM, HIS johnny crumpled at his neck. "He looks so young," Meryl whispered, her eyes filled with tears.

"That's because he is," Joe replied in a soft voice.

"He's just fallen asleep," the nurse said, stepping to the door. "I'll be back to check on him soon."

Meryl pulled up a chair nearer to the bed and Joe stood behind her, hand on her shoulder. After a minute or two of staring at her sleeping nephew, she looked up at him, dry-eyed. "It's okay, I'm okay, if you want to pop out for the clothes?"

"I can go to the clothing store up the street for things I know will fit him, if you prefer?"

She gave him a weary smile. "Your clothes will be fine. Thanks.

And would you mind stopping by the emergency room to find Johnny and Gigi? They were about to put a cast on her wrist when I left them. Please let them know what's going on."

"No worries. Can I bring anything back for you?"

"Just yourself," she said softly, placing her hand on his forearm. "Thank you."

SHORTLY AFTER JOE'S DEPARTURE, KIP WOKE UP AND PULLED HIS HAND from Meryl's. She looked up and smiled. "You're back."

"What happened?"

"It appears that one of your friends slipped you a mickey."

"What?"

"Old expression, sorry. Somehow, you ingested oxycodone. Do you remember taking something?"

He shook his head. "All we had at Rusty's were sodas."

"One of the kids put something in yours."

As Kip sat up, staring straight ahead, the door opened, and Johnny and Gigi came in. She ran to the bed and threw herself on her brother. "Thank God. I was so scared, Kip."

Her brother looked uncomfortable with her effusive embrace, but he patted her back. "Hey, Gi, I'm fine. It's cool."

"No, it is not cool," Johnny said, frowning as he approached the bed. "Large doses of oxycodone kill. Sometimes instantly. You were very lucky."

Meryl reached out and pinched her brother's arm. "He didn't know. One of the boys put it in his drink."

"That kid should be arrested and charged," Johnny said. "By the way, Richard says the police are on the way. They need to take both the kids' statements."

Meryl looked up at him. "Okay. Joe went to get Kip some fresh clothes."

"Yup, we saw him. He should be back soon."

CHAPTER 22

Johnny made dinner, grilled salmon, new potatoes, and asparagus, and Joe drove into town and got ice cream. Exhausted, Gigi and Kip wanted to watch a movie. After cleaning up, Johnny joined them, and Meryl and Joe decided to take a walk.

"I shouldn't go far," she said as they headed down Beach Road toward the Point. "I want to talk with them. I wish their mother would call."

Arm around her shoulder, he pulled her closer. Joe loved her familiar scent of citrus and beach roses. "They're gonna be fine. My guess is all of them will learn from this, especially the Corcoran boy."

"What do you think will happen to him?"

"At the least a warning, maybe some community service if it's his first offense. If Kip had been seriously hurt, it would have been much worse. Juvenile detention would probably be mandatory. May well be now."

Meryl sighed, leaning into him. "What a mess."

They walked in silence for a minute or two, then she paused and looked up at him. "How are you? Has the retreat been what you hoped?"

"In terms of a break, a chance to slow down and pause, it's been useful."

"That's a good thing, right?"

"I've missed you. That clouded everything."

"Oh, Joe, I'm sorry."

"Sorry? For what?"

"You're distracted because of me."

He laughed, kissing the top of her head. "My beautiful girl. Clouded may have been the wrong word. Thoughts of you have made things clearer, not cloudy. It's all the rest."

"Let's sit," she said, indicating one of several benches in a small greenspace that looked out toward Barnum's Ledge. Once seated side by side, she turned to him. "I'm confused."

"Me too. The priesthood had many ups and downs, but I knew my place, my role. I knew I was meant to offer compassion, comfort, and solace to my parishioners. To be there when they needed me, to teach the Gospel, to perform rites, rituals, and ceremonies, to administer the sacrament. Small town priesthood, even embedded in the rites and rituals of the Catholic church, can be more local, aimed at creating a community of supportive others beyond the tenets of the high church. At least that's been my experience. It's also a calling, which comes with the expectation of lifelong commitment. Or at least that's what I always believed.

"I left St. Mary's and my role as a priest with a peaceful heart, knowing it was what I wanted. I am grateful for my growing counseling practice as it allows me to continue a job where I'm a compassionate listener for clients, helping to bring them a measure of peace. What I hadn't anticipated were the broader parameters of a secular life—relationships, day-to-day interactions, love. In the absence of God and spiritual guidance, I'm not sure I know how to be compassionate to myself as I navigate this new life. All the familiar structures and routines have been washed away, and I'm adrift."

She took his hand. "I'm not Catholic, but I would think that God isn't absent for you now. His spiritual guidance will always be there, won't it? It's the new structures and routines that will take time to build, right?"

He nodded, his dark eyes gazing at her in the growing twilight. "You're such a wise, compassionate woman, my dear. Yes, building new life patterns will take time. That's what I'm learning, along with shouldering a healthy dose of Christian guilt. I've abandoned a life of service for a more selfish existence."

Meryl frowned. "Not necessarily."

He smiled, kissing her gently. "Of course, there is worthy service outside of the church. I know this rationally, but the years have told a different story."

She kissed him back, and she turned and circled her arms around his neck, drawing closer. All her senses aroused, she gave herself to him as his hands moved from her neck to her breasts. "Oh Joe, I've missed you so."

"I've missed you too. This sensual world you've opened up to me and so much more. Right now, my body tells me to tear your clothes off, mine too, and make wild, carnal love to you. At the same time, my mind is wracked with guilt for taking such pleasure for myself and for ravaging you."

"Oh, my love," she said, reaching up, her hands cradling his strong, handsome face. "If you haven't noticed by now, there's no ravaging going on. I'm a full participant in this carnal lovemaking, as you call it. My body bursts into flames whenever I see you. I would happily make love to you day and night it wasn't for jobs and life's responsibilities. There's no ravaging, I assure you, unless you think I'm ravaging you."

He laughed, taking her hands and kissing each palm. "My thinking isn't rational. I'm sorry."

"So, what shall we do now? Find a secluded spot and ravage each other?" she said.

"Tempting as that sounds, I think you need to get home and I need to be on my way."

"To?"

"I'm returning to Maine. For at least a week. Not as long as planned, but I need a little more time."

"Of course," she said, standing up, the breeze chilling her without his body beside her.

"You're angry," he said, rising, his hand cupping her chin.

"No, just tired and you're right, I should get back to the kids, if only to watch the tail end of the silly movie my brother picked out."

"I'm sorry I can't be more decisive, Meryl."

She took his hand, and they started walking back. "I understand. You need time." But did she really understand? *Will he return in a week or so and decide that our relationship was selfish and somehow wrong?*

After he said goodbye to Johnny and the kids, Meryl walked him to the truck. "Thank you for coming. It means the world to me."

"I wouldn't have been anywhere else. Take care, my darling." He kissed her, then opened the truck door and slid in. "Phone service is sketchy or nonexistent at the Arbors, but I'll try to send a message or two."

"This is your time," she said, stepping back. "Use it to focus on you and ways you can cultivate loving kindness for yourself going forward."

"Goodbye, Meryl," he said as he started the truck.

"Bye," she said, her heart aching with sadness as he backed up and drove away.

CHAPTER 23

Arbor residents could order meals boxed for pickup should they wish to eat in their cabins. Following his trip to Horseshoe Crab Cove, Joe ordered several days of meals and spent his time in solitude. After two days of eating alone, mostly sitting on the cabin porch gazing out at the sea, he decided it was time for company again. He'd seen Lilibet and George in passing, as well as some of the other residents with whom he'd become acquainted, but hadn't stopped to talk. There was a deep respect for one another in this peaceful spot, for which he was profoundly grateful. After forty-eight hours in silence and solitude, he headed up to the main building for supper with a smile on his face.

"Wonderful to see you, my boy," George said as Joe approached with his dinner tray.

"May I join you?" Joe asked, looking from George to Lilibet and two others with whom they sat.

She smiled, patting the empty chair beside her. "Of course, we'd love it. We've missed you." She introduced the couple beside them. Lorna and Tom, husband and wife, it turned out. After several minutes, the pair rose and said good night.

"Nice couple," George said. "Got here yesterday."

"How are you both?" Joe asked, gazing at his companions.

Lilibet smiled. "Enjoying the solitude, while marshaling my defenses for my future. I have five more months to accomplish this. My kids are begging to visit."

"Oh?" Joe said.

"Don't let 'em," George said, waving his fork with a large chunk of sweet potato on the end. "This is your time."

"Do you have an opinion, Joe?" she asked, her blue-gray eyes trained on him.

He shrugged. "I've just begun living in the real world. My only advice would be listen to your heart. It'll tell you what you want."

"Absolutely!" George said. "So how was your visit home?"

"Short, but it was good to see Meryl and the kids. I was glad I went."

George set down his fork. "If you don't mind me asking, was it the desire for marriage, family, a wife what made you decide to leave the priesthood?"

"Partially, but I also had an unsettling experience about a year before I stepped away." His companions waited, allowing him to decide if he wished to explain further. "I was asked to participate in a synod with some of my colleagues in the city. Our task was to research and examine a vibrant Catholic faith community of which the archdiocese didn't approve, and which the church leaders thought should be disbanded. It was a small but very committed group of about seventy-five members. Devout Catholics who were very involved in their local community. They all volunteered in countless charitable organizations. This service was at the core of their faith. Their very human, spiritual faith.

"I spent many months with them, attending services when I could, talking to the elders and many others. The issue for the bishop was their divergence from the traditional liturgy and their unconventional mass. He didn't consider their Sunday mass Catholic, but something else entirely. He'd admonished them many times over their years of existence, but while Catholicism was at the core of their life, they were also committed to a humane spiritualism. Our task was to decide if they could continue as a Catholic church community or whether they should be shut down.

"It was a wrenching process, but in the end, our group recommended to the archdiocese that they be forbidden to call themselves a Catholic community. They were heartbroken, but without the sanction of their Catholic leadership, they elected to disband."

"How sad," she said.

"That's exactly why I'm a lapsed Catholic," George said, shaking his head. "Bunch of shortsighted idiots."

"George!" she said, giving him a sharp look.

Joe smiled. "It's okay. I've heard worse said about the church. I was not in favor of nor did I vote for closure, so I went home discouraged and disillusioned. I never really recovered. Still haven't."

On the kids' last full day, Meryl had to work in the afternoon, but she was taking the evening off. Gigi asked to come to Field and Fire with her, and she was now chopping vegetables at Cady's side. Johnny and Kip were having a "guys' day," which involved watching several mindless movies and fishing off the dock. Brother and sister had spent the last few days entertaining them, taking day trips to Sturbridge Village, Plymouth Plantation, and Manomet Bird Sanctuary. She could tell the trips had been somewhat boring for Kip and Gigi but decided that boredom might be relaxing after their ordeal with the Corcorans. A great lunch somewhere along the way boosted their spirits, and the four came home to dinner at Meryl's, a restaurant in town, or one evening at Morgan's Fire. Tonight, they were eating at home.

As she went over the day's menus with Rori and Freddy, the back door slammed open and Lyddie came in, red-faced, tears streaking her cheeks.

"Hey, baby, what's wrong?" Rori asked.

"Nothing." Lyddie headed into the storeroom where staff members had lockers.

Rori rolled her eyes, then returned her attention to her companions. "Best to leave her to cool down, but this is getting ridiculous. What's the matter with Wolfie Morgan?" she whispered. "Either make a decision or cut her loose."

Freddy leaned closer to them. "It's a two-way street. I believe our Lydia may be a bit of a spoiled princess."

Meryl looked at him. "She's never impressed me that way. Maybe they jumped into things too quickly?"

Lyddie reappeared, buttoning the top buttons of her white shirt and grabbing an apron. "I'm here earlier than expected. Put me to work."

Rori stood up and crooked her finger. "Come along. I have just the job for you, babe." She exchanged looks with Meryl and Freddie as she swung open the dining room door. "Be right back."

"So, you've had quite the week, haven't you?" Freddie said.

"Yes... It's been a roller coaster. I've actually enjoyed my visitors, but I'll be glad to get back to familiar routines."

"Rori says the big boss is holding a meeting next week to discuss workload. Do you know anything about that?"

She shrugged. "I know he's committed to all of us having a life, so I'm guessing it's not about increasing our hours."

"Fingers crossed," he said as Rori rejoined them.

Meryl looked up at her head chef. "So what's the meeting about next week? I've barely seen Sandy."

"Flexible work hours. Not sure how he's envisioning this, but he mentioned it to me. I'm sure Murph knows more since he tells him and you more than he does me."

"I doubt that. Now, back to tonight's menus," Meryl said, shuffling bits of notes and paper where she'd jotted ideas.

They were soon interrupted again, this time by Wolfie, who knocked, then pushed open the back door. "Lyddie here?"

"In the dining room." Rori nodded toward the door behind her. "Killing time before the dinner rush begins."

"Thanks," he said, nodding as he headed by them for the door. Richard's youngest had always reminded Meryl of a swashbuckler, with his long dark hair, beard, and coal-black eyes. While she didn't know him well, she liked him. She hoped that the young couple would resolve things. They were beautiful to see together when things were going well.

Rori shook her head. "Fingers crossed. I really hate drama, especially in the workplace."

WOLFIE FOUND HER SETTING THE TABLES IN THE SMALL DINING ROOM, IN preparation for a private party. "Hey, Lyd, can we talk?" Wolfie asked.

"I'm busy."

"No, you're not. Rori says you're just killing time."

Lyddie plunked a stack of pale pink linen napkins on a half-set table. "Fine."

A strand of her sandy-blonde hair broken loose from her ponytail and fell across her cheek. Wolfie sat beside her, fighting the urge to lean forward and smooth the errant locks back. To his eyes, she was the most beautiful woman he'd ever seen—her freckles and pale soft skin, her hazel eyes and slender, perfect figure. He loved her. He was sure of it, but he was also not ready to settle down, share a living space, all the rest.

He'd tried the live-in thing once during his early years at Northeastern, with a woman named Jane. It had ended in disaster. She'd thrown all his belongings out windows to the sidewalk in front of their Commonwealth Avenue apartment. He hadn't loved Jane, but she'd been fun and a good friend until demands for commitment arose. They were juniors and she wanted to get engaged. The thought hadn't even occurred to Wolfie, and he reacted with shock when she suggested it. That had been the beginning of the end.

"I'm sorry we argued. I think you know that I care very much for you."

Lyddie shrugged. "Do I?"

"People can care very much for someone, but not be ready to share a home. We're both still young."

"You mean I am."

"Wouldn't you rather finish college? Be independent for a while? I'm not going anywhere."

"Says you. Women practically throw themselves at you wherever we are."

"Not true, and even if it was, which it's not, the only woman I care about is you."

"You say that now, but two years from now, who knows?"

"Lyddie," he said, taking her hand, which he was gratified to see she didn't yank away. "Do you want to move in with me because you don't think we'll last otherwise?"

Tears rimmed her hazel eyes as she turned to him. "Yes."

"Oh, baby, it's not true. I love you. I'm just not ready for the rest. I want to really get the winery going, decide if this is even what I want, where I want to live, the whole thing."

"Why can't we decide those things together?"

"We can, but we don't have to live under the same roof. You're in Providence, I'm here."

She pulled her hand away from him and straightened up. "Okay... We've had this conversation a million times. I'm not doing it anymore. I've been offered a job in Providence for the summer, maybe continuing into next year. I'm going to take it. I love it here, near my dad and you, but I'm stuck. I don't want to be stuck anymore. I'm giving Sandy my notice tonight."

"Lyddie, this isn't what I want at all."

"No, it's what I want. Now I've got to set all these tables," she said, standing and turning her back on him.

"Can we at least have a meal together? Talk this through? Lunch? Dinner? Anything."

"I think we've said it all. I love you, but I've had enough."

Wolfie stood and watched her setting each napkin in its place, the set of her shoulders demonstrating her distress. He wanted to wrap her in his arms and beg her to stay, to give him more time, but he was pretty sure she'd rebuff him. "Okay then, good luck. If you feel like stopping by before you leave, give me a call." No response. "Bye, then," he said, walking away. Walking away from the woman he loved. *Maybe time apart will be helpful?* he thought, shrugging.

On his way out, he bumped into Sandy at the front door. "Hey, man, how's it going?" the restaurant owner asked. "Everything okay?"

"Not my best day," Wolfie replied.

"Want to talk about it?"

"Thanks, but not now. See you later when we bring over the wine. Need anything in town?"

"Not that I can think of. Later."

Wolfie pushed open the door and headed for his Land Rover, a recent purchase made possible because he had virtually no expenses living at the farm with his father and Lucy. *Yes,* he thought, wrenching open the Rover's door. *Maybe time apart is what we need? I miss her already.*

CHAPTER 24

"Okay, now let's pretend I'm a woman you've seen or met and want to get to know," Lilibet said. Over lunch, the three friends had arranged to meet in the field outside her cabin to practice ways to make approaching women less fearful for George. "Joe will demonstrate how to approach me, then you can try."

Joe laughed, throwing up his arms. "As if an ex-priest knows anything about courting!"

"Well, first off, the term courting is rarely used anymore. I'd advise against it. Now, you've told us yourself that you're in the middle of a passionate love affair. You must have some idea how it's done. In fact, as a relative neophyte, you might be better giving advice than an experienced lothario. Now, come on. Give it a try."

Joe stepped forward and said, "Hello. Ms. Jones, so nice to see you. How are you?"

"Very well, but please call me Sally."

"And I'm Joe. I've seen you around town and have thought how nice it would be to get to know you better. Could I buy you a cup of coffee or tea sometime?"

"I'd like that, thank you. Would you be free now?" She turned to George. "See? That's a simple ice breaker. If you try it and it works, great. If not, you try something else. Shall we try it?"

They spent several hours, much of the time spent laughing, as they acted out a number of scenarios. As the sun faded behind the trees, George thanked them both, pronounced himself hopeless, and set off for afternoon yoga. His companions waved him off, then went to their cabins to change for yoga.

Later at dinner, when they were still in their yoga clothes, Lilibet set down her fork and said, "I think we made progress today, don't you, Joe?"

"Absolutely. By the end, you were very smooth and natural, George. Smoother than I've ever been."

"Oh, stuff and bother, you two. You can't fool me."

"I meant what I said," Joe said, patting his shoulder.

"As you yourself said, what does an ex-priest know about courting?"

Lilibet cringed. "There's that word again! Dating, hanging out, see each other, even hooking up is preferable to courting."

"Maybe not for my generation," George said. "After all, I don't want to date a young chickie."

She rolled her eyes. "That word won't get you far either. Now, back to the dating game. We ran off to yoga so fast that I forgot to give you your homework."

George looked over at her, eyes wide. "Homework?"

"Of course. If we're going to take this seriously and get you anywhere, you have to practice outside of class. Your homework is to find someone here, introduce yourself, and ask them to share tea or a meal with you."

"Don't be ridiculous. People come here to get away, to retreat. The last thing they want is to be asked on a date."

She smiled, exchanging looks with Joe. "You'd be surprised. Anyway, there's always the option for a woman to say 'no, thank you.' It's not the end of the world. If you want people to hang out with, you still have Joe and me. In fact, maybe if you zero in on someone, you could use me to make her think other women are after you? Of course, that's down the line."

Joe chuckled. "And probably ill-advised for many reasons."

Lilibet shrugged. "You're probably right. I've been married for most of my life. What do I know about dating either, but George, I'll make you a deal. If you try your moves on someone, I will too. We can't ask Joe to do it because he's with Meryl, but you and I are swinging singles, so what do we have to lose?"

"Our dignity, for one thing," he said, pushing a string bean around his plate.

"Then it's settled. We'll give it a day and reconnoiter at dinner tomorrow to give our reports."

"What if this mythical woman and I decide to have dinner tomorrow evening?"

"Then we debrief at breakfast day after tomorrow." She clapped her hands, her cheeks rosy and flushed. "I love it when a plan comes together!"

"Heaven help us, huh, Joe?" George said.

"You'll do great," Joe said, standing. "Can I get anyone tea or dessert?"

"ALL PACKED?" MERYL ASKED AS THE FOUR OF THEM SAT AT BREAKFAST. It was a warm, sunny morning, and they were eating on her porch overlooking the water. "Your mom should be here in an hour or so."

"Why the long faces?" Johnny asked, catching his sister's eye.

"We don't want to go," Gigi said. She took a piece of toast and slathered it with butter and strawberry preserves.

"It's boring at home," Kip said, "And we'll have to go back to school. We'll have so much work to make up."

"That's how vacations work," Johnny said. "They happen, they're great, then you go back to real life."

"Real life sucks," Kip said, pushing his plate away and gazing out at the river.

"No, it doesn't," Gigi said, "Except for the hospital and all, this time has been so awesome, and I don't even care about the missed schoolwork. I did most of the packets Mom sent us anyway."

Kip rolled his eyes. "Still sucks."

"Reentry can be tough," Meryl said. "I've loved my days off to be with you guys. And if your mom says yes, you can visit again."

"Yeah, but we're always on the move. Who knows where she'll drag us next now that Roger's in the picture."

"What do you do about school anyway?" Johnny asked.

"She gets all this homeschooling shit and makes us do it for five hours a day," Kip said. "I'm sick of it."

A knock at the door interrupted them, and Meryl rose to answer. When she opened the door, three strangers stood on the doorstep. A man, a woman, and a familiar boy about Kip's age. The man nodded. "Hello, I'm Mark Corcoran, and this is my wife, Sue. I think you know our boy, Rusty."

"I've seen him from afar at Pony Camp, yes," she answered.

Rusty's father adjusted his tie, a nervous gesture since it was perfectly smooth, along with his charcoal gray suit, crisp white dress shirt and coifed brown hair. "May we come in?"

"Of course." Meryl stood aside to allow them to pass.

Rusty's mother was dressed more casually in beige slacks and a patterned cotton sweater swirling with red poppies. Her blonde hair fell at her shoulders, her makeup tasteful, but obvious, especially the thick black eyelashes that overwhelmed her green eyes. Her son, redheaded and freckled, was dressed in jeans and a T-shirt. He kept his head down as his father nudged him forward.

"Oh, dear, we've interrupted your meal," Sue said, gazing at the porch and the three stunned diners looking in at them.

"No worries, we were just finishing," Meryl said. "Would you like to sit down?"

"Thank you, but this won't take long," Mark said. With Rusty in tow, he moved to stand at the doorway leading to the porch. "Rusty?"

The boy looked up. "I'm sorry, Kip and Gigi. Mostly Kip. I never should have... Well, I know it was wrong to stick that stuff in your soda without telling you."

Kip shrugged. "I'm okay now."

"Mr. and Ms. Stockdale, please accept the apology of our entire family. If there were any hospital costs incurred for either of your children, we will reimburse you in full."

"Gigi and Kip are our niece and nephew," Meryl said, "And this is my brother, Johnny. Thank you. When I get an accounting from the hospital, I'll forward it to you." *Only fair since your son almost killed my nephew!*

"We're really, truly sorry," Sue said. "It's the first time we left the kids on their own, and Markie and Leonie were supposed to be looking out for them. They're our oldest."

"Well...it's over," Meryl said. "Kip and Gigi's mom is coming soon to take them home."

"Okay, then, we won't take any more of your time. Nice to meet you all," Mark said, hand still resting on his son's shoulder as they pivoted from the doorway.

Johnny and the kids stayed seated as Meryl walked them to the door. Father and son stepped out first, and Sue turned to her. "No hard feelings, I hope? We love your restaurant, and I hear the new menu is to die for."

"Thank you," Meryl replied. "Take care." She watched the trio descend the steps and head to a black Mercedes SUV, then went back inside.

"Well, that was something," Johnny said as she rejoined them at the table.

"Some kind of something indeed," she said. "You guys okay?"

They nodded.

"Rusty didn't look too happy," Gigi said.

"From what I hear, he's facing criminal charges," Meryl said. "I imagine he's scared to death, even though someone told me his dad's an attorney."

"Parents were certainly a pair," Johnny said. "I mean, her sweater and that makeup! Ghoulish!"

Meryl suppressed a smile. "She's apparently a very successful interior decorator. Has a shop in Southport."

Johnny rolled his eyes. "With that getup, she probably scares customers away."

~

AN HOUR LATER, SHERRY ARRIVED IN A FLURRY. "OH, MY BABIES!" SHE cried, hugging and kissing them. By the kids' reactions, Meryl surmised that they weren't accustomed to such effusive greetings.

A handsome woman rather than a conventional beauty, Sherry had a wiry athletic build, sky-blue eyes, and dirty blonde hair pulled into a long braid down her back. Deeply tan, Sherry had very large breasts for her body. Johnny called them a "cosmetic miracle." After embracing the kids and sending them off to collect their bags, she turned to her half brother and sister.

"So? Anything I need to know?"

Meryl grabbed a blue folder from the kitchen counter. "They've both been given a clean bill of health by the hospital doctors. Gigi's cast should come off in six weeks, but the orthopedist said you can go to your home doctor for that. All their records are in here. The Corcorans have offered to pay all medical expenses, including for Gigi's wrist, and given the circumstances, I accepted. If I receive any further paperwork here, I'll forward it to him and you. I've made copies of everything in the folder and will send the invoices I have now to them this afternoon, unless you'd like to take it all with you and send it to the Corcorans? Their contact information is in there as well."

Sherry leafed through the folder, then looked up. "Why don't you go ahead and send it, then I'll follow up after the cast removal. So, what about suing? That was the first thing Roger said. I should sue the bastards."

Meryl and Johnny exchanged looks, then he said, "That's your call, Sherry."

"No, Mom, you're not suing!" Kip said as he dropped his duffels near the front door. "It was an accident."

"The hell it was!" she said, hands on hips.

"If you sue, I'll say I took the pills voluntarily."

"The boy's facing criminal charges, Sherry. That may be punishment enough."

"Whatever, we'll see. These are my precious angels after all. Kip, take your sister's bags. She can't do it with her cast."

As they headed out, Sherry turned to Meryl. "Thanks so much for taking them. The past three weeks were heaven."

Meryl smiled. "It was a pleasure. The hospital detour aside, I think they enjoyed themselves."

"Don't I know it. They've been texting the past few days begging to stay longer."

"Anytime," Meryl said. "It's a great place for kids, and I hear the summer's incredible. This is my first one here."

"Maybe Roger and I'll come on vacation. Are there decent hotels in the area?"

Meryl nodded. "A brand new inn."

"A fancy spa," Johnny added.

"And lots of B-and-Bs and motels in the area," she said.

"Plus, we've got to try your restaurant," Sherry said. "The buzz about it is all over social media."

"We've been lucky," she said.

"Well, ta-ta, then."

Sherry traipsed down to join the kids by her battered old jeep. Meryl and Johnny followed, hugging both kids, all with tears in their eyes. "Come back anytime," she said to both.

"I'll plan to come back too," Johnny said.

Then the jeep pulled away, hands and arms waving from the windows. Meryl turned to her brother. "It'll be good to get back to normal, but I'll miss them and you."

"Ditto, sis."

"What time's your flight?"

"Two. The Uber's arriving in an hour."

"I told you I'd take you."

"I'm fine. Time to put your feet up for a few hours and dream of gorgeous Joe."

"Dream is right."

"What's happened to the optimistic sister I know and love?"

Meryl leaned against his shoulder as they headed back inside. "Life and a healthy dose of realism, I guess."

"Realism's overrated," he replied, slipping an arm around her shoulders. "Prince Charming is crazy about you."

Prince Charming indeed, she thought, smiling despite her aching heart.

CHAPTER 25

Time went by in a blur for Meryl, the restaurant hopping as she endeavored to catch up after the kids' visit and her days off. She missed Johnny and his cheerful banter and wished they lived closer. Joe called a few times, but they never connected. She vacillated between despair and hope when thinking about him. His voicemails were short, and he sounded distracted. Since he'd told her his phone was locked up in the office most of the time, she knew she couldn't call him back.

"This isn't the face of the most successful chef in New England right now," Sandy said, when he found her in the office Saturday at noon. Meryl was hunched over, finalizing the day's menus and moping about Joe.

She gave him a weary smile. "You, of course, know that my success is mostly due to you."

"Not true. Now what's wrong? You look like you just lost your best friend." Her boss's gorgeous dark eyes studied her closely. Sandy hated it when his employees and colleagues were unhappy.

"I think I may have," she said, setting the menus aside.

"I'm guessing this friend is the handsome Mr. O'Leary. What's going on, if you don't mind my asking?"

"Still transitioning to the secular life. He's been a priest for most of his life."

Sandy smiled. "My parents tried to bring us up in the Catholic church—CCD, the whole nine yards. It didn't take, and they're so busy with the restaurant, they don't get to mass very often. A whole lot of guilt built up over the years. Takes a while to process when you step away from a spiritualism that has ruled most of your existence. For our mom especially, the church was and is a great source of comfort."

"I'm sure," Meryl said. "I think Joe misses comforting others, caring for his parishioners."

"He sure saved the O'Neills' lives when Murph's sister died. After Aislan's accident, he was at the house day and night."

"I think he's endeavoring to bring that same caring and solace to people in his counseling practice, but there's a difference, a distance that some of his former parishioners can't accept or understand. They want Father Joe, not a lay therapist."

"They'll adjust. It hasn't even been a year, has it?"

"No."

"Hey, you doing anything tomorrow night? My father-in-law and Lucy are having one of their Sunday night suppers, cast of thousands and all. Pam and I are going, Murph and Greta too. Why don't you come? They'd love to have you."

"I don't want to intrude on a family thing."

"Did you not hear the 'cast of thousands' part? I'll add your name to the list. We'll swing by and pick you up. Around five?"

"Are you sure?"

"Wouldn't have asked if I wasn't."

"Thank you. I'd love to come."

"Now let's get through tonight. We're booked solid from four thirty to ten. We may have to rethink take-out on Saturdays. It's getting too crazy."

"I agree. That's on my list for our next staff meeting."

Sandy stood. "Want me to get someone to send the menus off? We can print 'em in town if you're swamped."

"No, take me ten minutes."

"Okay, then," he said, then headed toward the dining room.

"Sandy?" she said, as he pushed the door open. "Thanks."

He gave her one of his glorious smiles, the ones that made women go weak at the knees. "No problem."

No problem indeed, Meryl mused, opening her laptop. She decided to type up the menu herself, then emailed it to the print shop in town. The shop printed them on special paper and delivered them by three in the afternoon.

CHAPTER 26

"So glad you could join us, Meryl," Richard said, his arm circled around her shoulders. "Lucy and I are always saying we should see more of you and Joe. How is he, anyway? We heard he was away."

"He's fine as far as I know. The retreat center where he's staying discourages phones and computer use, except if you're there to work on your writing. He'll be back this Wednesday to officiate at Murph and Greta's wedding."

"Terrific. We're thrilled the youngsters decided to have the reception at Field and Fire. Beautiful venue with the water views and your spectacular cuisine. They are such a cute couple, aren't they?" he said, gesturing across the room at Murph and Greta, who were chatting with Lucy's sister, Harriet, and her husband, Kyle.

"Yes, they are."

"Will you get to enjoy some of the party, I hope?"

Meryl smiled at her gregarious host. "I'll enjoy everyone enjoying themselves and our food."

"You'll certainly join in the champagne toast and dancing after dessert?"

"I'll try."

"Dad, you're needed in the kitchen," Pam said, appearing from the front hall. "Callie has a question," she added, referring to the Morgans' housekeeper and cook.

He looked at his daughter in surprise. "And you couldn't relay it?"

Pam smiled, winking at Meryl. "Apparently not. Now chop chop."

With one squeeze of her shoulders, he headed for the kitchen, greeting people along the way.

"Your father's something, isn't he?" Meryl said.

"Hmm."

"Callie doesn't need him, does she?"

Pam grinned. "I thought you needed rescuing. Besides, I've been meaning to check in and see how you are post kids' visit, with Joe away and all."

"I loved having Kip and Gigi. Every minute of it. It helped to have my brother here too. We don't get to see each other often enough. Joe? Who knows? Things have been up and down with us. He's still getting his bearing in his post-priesthood life."

"Sandy mentioned something."

Meryl shrugged, taking a sip of her excellent Morgan's Fire sauvignon blanc. "He was great when the kids had that bit of trouble. Left the retreat and came down for the day to lend support. As for the rest... When you care about someone and they're struggling, you give them support and space."

"He's lucky to have you. I don't know Joe well, but he impresses me as a wonderful man. It must be a shock to spend so many years secluded, on your own and devoted to God, then be thrust into life in this active, buzzing community. His day-to-day life must be so different for him now."

"Yes," Meryl said, as Richard called them to dinner by ringing a brass cow bell.

"Where did you get that stupid thing?" Weezie asked, rolling her eyes.

Her father grinned. "Pretty nifty, huh?"

Lucy stood at his side, shaking her head. "I'll work on sneaking it down to the barn soon," she said, reaching over to take her husband's hand.

A loving couple, Meryl thought as she always did when she saw Richard and Lucy together, their large, wonderful family surrounding them.

As always, dinner was a lively, raucous affair. It was a smaller crowd than usual tonight, since Richard's daughter Ava and her family were away, and Rich, Karen, Tim, and Gail were at Land's End, eating with the Millers, Karen and Tim's family. Wolfie and Lyddie were out at Barnum's Ledge eating with Lolly and Jack. Meryl sat across from Weezie, flanked by Greta on one side and Murph on the other. She'd offered to move to allow the couple to sit side by side, but they had pooh-poohed her, insisting that they'd be spending lots of time side by side in future.

Weezie kept up most of the conversation, telling them the latest at the stables and pony camp. "I had such a great time with Kip and Gigi," she said. "They are two terrific kids. Too bad they don't live locally, because I'd hire them in a couple of years to be my counselors or assistants."

"Oh?" Meryl said.

"Yeah, Amy helps out, and she's loved going out to Saguaro to live with our aunt and uncle during the summers she's worked at their camp, Emma's Dream. It's a great job for teenagers who love kids and horses."

Meryl smiled, thinking how over the moon Kip and Gigi would be at such an opportunity. "I'm sure they'd be thrilled."

As always, Callie's food was extraordinary. Tonight, since both of Lucy's kids, Rob and Amy, were with them, Callie followed one of their family's Sunday traditions and, after taking orders, had made a variety of pizzas with all kinds of toppings as well as a colorful field greens salad. Sated from dinner and dessert, Meryl walked to her car alongside Greta and Murph. She realized she felt peaceful for the first time in weeks. Whatever happened with Joe, she knew they would remain friends. *That's a comfort anyway*, she mused.

As the three said good night, Greta turned to her. "What would be a good time for me to stop by the restaurant and finalize the menus for Saturday?"

"Would Wednesday afternoon suit you? That would give us time to order any additional items," Meryl replied. "Around three? Will you be out of work by that time?"

"Perfect. The school's letting me work half days this week, so my caseload's small. Barring any emergency, three on Wednesday should work fine."

"It's a date," she said, turning to her colleague. "Will the groom be joining us?"

Murph grinned. "I'm assuming you're meeting at the restaurant, right? I'll poke my head in, if that's okay?"

"Of course, it's okay," Greta said, winking at Meryl. "See you then, Meryl."

"Night," she said as she opened her car door. *They really are a cute couple*, she thought, waving one last time.

"It's been an interesting three weeks," Joe said to Lilibet and George Wednesday morning of their last breakfast together. "No, interesting just scratches the surface. Spending time with you both has been spiritually affirming and nurturing in ways I can't express. It's also been great fun. Thank you."

She smiled. "Taking ourselves out of our daily lives often helps us to reenter them in a fuller, more expansive way. Dare I say that we learn how to live by stepping out of life?"

"You can say what ya like," George said. "I'm gonna miss this kid. Maybe I'll make a move to that village of his. I retire from teaching a year after this sabbatical, so I'll be free as a bird."

"I would love that," Joe said.

"Maybe you can scout around and find me a nice lady friend?"

"I'll get right on that. You would both be welcome to come and stay anytime. My rental house has three bedrooms, so there's plenty of room and there are a variety of great accommodations in town as well."

"Maybe a reunion when I leave here next fall?" Lilibet said.

"Sounds great," Joe said. "I'm sure Meryl would love to meet you both."

George raised his coffee cup in toast. "Very hopeful talk, that?"

Joe smiled, looking from one to the other. "Not sure what our status will be, but I know with certainty that we will be friends, good friends."

"And much more," Lilibet said. "I'm sure of it. You're a wonderful man, Joe O'Leary." The three had shared surnames and contact information a few days earlier. "Any woman would be fortunate to create a loving partnership with you. Your spiritualism gives you a depth and compassion that you bring to any relationship, including this one," she added, gesturing around at the three of them. "People are blessed to fall under your arc."

"Thank you, friends. Your kind words mean a great deal."

"Have you time for one more walk along the cliffs?" George asked.

"Of course," he replied, thinking about Lilibet's words about stepping back into his life, if not transformed, at least clearer about what that life might be. *Whatever happens, I know this is the life I want moving forward and that life must include Meryl, if she'll still have anything to do with me.*

CHAPTER 27

Murph and Greta had decided on an informal reception, no sit-down dinner, just finger foods hot and cold. The food and one of two bars would be outside on the new enclosed veranda at the south end of the restaurant. Dancing and dessert would happen inside in the smaller, south-facing dining room, where doors would be opened to the veranda.

After several discussions with Meryl about what to serve, they decided on skewers of shrimp and lamb, lobster and chicken salad tea sandwiches, pork sliders, and ribs. It was an eclectic menu composed of their favorites and some of Meryl's suggestions. She recommended that they add some vegan choices in addition to the crudites, chopped salad, and Caesar salad wonton cups. Cady offered a variety of dip choices—baba ghanoush, almond cheese, Field and Fire guacamole, and beet muhammara. She also planned to serve mango nori wraps, carrot ginger gyoza dumplings, and several kinds of bruschetta.

As the two women sat talking Wednesday afternoon, Greta met Meryl's eyes. "Do you think it's too much?"

Meryl peered over her reading glasses and smiled. "It sounds like a lot, but remember, most everything except for a few of the hot appetizers will be on tables or stations around the veranda. We'll arrange the meat choices on one, vegan and dips at another, and of course the towering, multi-level charcuterie board, which will need its own table."

Greta shook her head. "That's what I mean! My fiancé and his ribs, sliders, and ridiculous cheese tower."

"You have seventy-five guests. Things will disappear fast."

"I guess so. When is Fiona bringing the cake? Did she say?" Murph's mother was creating an Irish wedding cake of raisins, currants, candied cherries, almonds, citrus peel, molasses, and heady spices such as nutmeg and ginger. Field and Fire's pastry chef was also making signature cookies and squares for people who didn't care for heavy fruitcake. At the last minute, Fiona agreed to omit the traditional soaking in whiskey or rum in deference to her husband, a recovering alcoholic. Breads and rolls would be coming from Moon and Stars.

Meryl looked at her notes. "She said she'd drop it off Saturday morning."

"And the edible desserts are all set too, right?" Greta asked as her fiancé walked into the dining room.

"I heard that. Mom's fruitcake is dry, but perfectly edible."

"For some people," Greta said, glancing over at Meryl.

"How you ladies doing?"

"Great, almost done," Meryl said. "Do you want to look things over? Add anything?"

"As long as my sliders, ribs, and cheese tower are still there, I'm good." He turned to Meryl. "Hey, I just saw Joe at the house. Looks good. Sounds like he had a great getaway." Joe rented Murph's house in Southport, and his landlord stopped in to check on things at least once a week.

"How was he?" Greta asked.

"Same ole Joe. He's all set with the ceremony. He's gonna drive down and talk with Belle tomorrow or Friday. Belle's the Clerk of the Meeting," he added for Meryl's benefit. "You okay, Chef? You look a little green around the gills."

"I'm fine," she replied. "Just need to eat something before the evening rush."

"Oh, of course," Greta said, hopping up. "I'm sorry I've kept you so long."

Meryl hugged her. "No worries. This is fun stuff. You're going to have a beautiful day."

AFTER UNPACKING, JOE MADE A SMALL LIST AND HEADED FOR THE market in Southport. Once back home, he put away his groceries and took a beer to the back porch. He loved the rickety old porch and often sat reading in the evenings now that the weather had warmed. May was his favorite month, with everything blooming and the promise of summer just around the corner. He opened his book, a new mystery by a writer he greatly admired, then sighed. Closing the book, he set it on the wooden lobster pot that Murph used as a table.

Meryl... It was always Meryl who occupied his thoughts during quiet moments. For years, his world had been focused on the concerns of his parishioners. If he wasn't counseling them, conducting mass, or visiting them at home, hospital, or care facility, his thoughts dwelled on them, their joys, sorrows, and complaints, and ways he could assist, support, and comfort them. Now the quiet moments focused on Meryl. At fifty, he finally knew what romantic love for another human being felt like. He burned for her physically and emotionally. He missed their talks and her calm, caring ways. He'd spent many hours in Maine talking with Lilibet, George, and a counselor about his guilt and whether the joy and happiness he felt with Meryl was selfish and wrong. His two retreat companions had repeatedly told him such thinking was crazy, and rationally, he knew it was.

"Oh, for goodness' sake!" he said aloud, standing, grabbing his book, and heading inside.

He grabbed his phone from the front hall table. She answered on the first ring. "Hello?"

How he loved the rich, throaty timbre of her voice. "Hi, it's me. I'm home."

"Hello... Yes, Murph told us he'd seen you."

"How are you?"

"Busy. Just taking a quick break on our new veranda before the dinner rush begins. How are you?"

"Well, thanks. I'd love to see you. Would you be free at all tomorrow?"

"There's so much to do for the wedding and the upcoming weekend. Maybe a few hours in the morning? Supposed to be a beautiful day. A walk? Nine-ish?"

"Perfect. Shall I come to you?"

"Why don't I come your way? I have to pick up a few things at Tishell's, the gourmet emporium in Southport. Do you know it?"

He chuckled. "Yes, a fun place to roam even if I don't know what half the stuff is." His body relaxed as they conversed about ordinary things.

"There's a walking path that runs behind Tishell's and then along the water. We could meet in the parking lot and walk from there?"

"Sounds good. Nine, then?"

"See you tomorrow. Glad you're safely home. Sleep well."

As Joe set down the phone, he felt more peaceful than he had in several days. *Now home feels real because she's in it*, he thought, going back to the kitchen to fix supper.

CHAPTER 28

The morning dawned bright and sunny with clear skies. Meryl showered, then gathered her things. She planned to go straight to the restaurant after her trip to Southport. There might be time to sneak home for a brief nap in the afternoon, but she grabbed clothes for the evening just in case she couldn't break away. Wolfie always made the partially furnished apartment above the tasting barn available to staff members should anyone wish to shower or rest during a hectic day. Meryl had only taken advantage of it once since arriving at Field and Fire, but maybe this was the day to call and see if it was available. She shoved toilet articles and her makeup bag into her backpack, just in case.

When she pulled into Tishell's lot, she spied Joe leaning against his truck. He waved. His gorgeous smile transformed his craggy features as he smoothed back a lock of thick salt-and-pepper hair from his eyes, then began walking toward her.

"Hello."

"Hello, Joe," she answered, falling into his outstretched arms. "It's so good to see you."

"You too." He bent to kiss her, a light, friendly kiss that sent waves of heat coursing through her.

"The path's around the back. Shall we?"

"Lead the way."

As they started off, their hands brushed and he took hers. They had always had a perfect walking rhythm when holding hands. No awkward steps. Just a smooth, completely synchronous motion as if they became one body. He asked about the restaurant and what she'd been up to and told her a little about his time in Maine and the friends he'd made.

The ocean was flat and calm below them as they made their way along the cliffs. About two miles later, she spied a large, flat boulder and suggested they sit before turning back. Side by side, still holding hands, they stared out at the sea, neither speaking for a minute or two. Finally, she said, "Was your time away helpful?"

"Yes."

"Are you more settled and at peace?"

He turned to meet her gaze. "It's a process."

Inwardly cringing, Meryl swallowed, then decided, *it's now or never*. "So, where is your thinking about us?"

"Honestly? All over the place. I know that I care very deeply for you and can't imagine not having you in my life. I missed you terribly." He reached over and smoothed hair from her forehead, a familiar, gentle gesture that she loved.

"I hear a 'but' in there," she said.

"No buts in terms of friendship. The rest? Not sure yet. Maybe a few steps back to reflect?"

Her heart ached, but inwardly, Meryl seethed. Her past relationships had usually ended with her partner's infidelity or boredom. Here she was again, with another man who couldn't get out from under himself. "I see." She stood up more abruptly than she intended, slipping her hand from his. "We better head back. I've got to get to work." She turned and began walking at a swift pace back the way they'd come.

"Meryl, wait!" he cried, following her down the path. Jogging to catch up with her, he grasped her arm. "Please stop. I'm sorry."

"I am too," she said, looking up with tears in her beautiful blue eyes.

"I'm so sorry if I've hurt you. That's the last thing I intended, but I wanted to be honest."

"And now you have been. I'm sorry too, but I can't do this anymore. Maybe someday when you figure things out, we can be friends. Right now, maybe we should step back, as you say. Not see each other for a while. Now, I really do have to get back."

They walked in silence, Meryl ahead of him until they reached the parking lot. She unlocked her car and grabbed her purse before turning back to him. "Time to shop."

"Do you need help?"

"No, I just need a few things, and I know right where they are. They've also put a box together for me." She leaned forward, giving him a quick hug. "Take care. Bye."

As he stood watching her enter the small grocery store, Joe knew he'd screwed up. *Big-time.* His heart ached, and he resolved to pray for guidance and clarity. He wanted to follow her. *But to follow is cruel*, he thought, turning to walk to his truck. *And I've already been cruel enough.*

CHAPTER 29

"I can't believe our boy's going to be married tomorrow," Fiona MacGregor O'Neill said. She clapped her hands and winked at Joe. "To the loveliest girl in the world."

"They are a beautiful couple." He stood with his host on the O'Neill's backyard terrace. It was a warm evening, and they were enjoying drinks outside before Fiona's dinner of traditional Dublin Coddle, field greens, and crusty breads. The dessert was Irish cream trifle. The coddle and trifle were Murph's favorites, approved by Greta, with a second small alcohol-free trifle created for her husband.

"And what about you, dear Joe? How is your beautiful relationship? I was surprised you didn't bring Meryl tonight."

"She's working."

"You must be thrilled to be home. I'm sure you missed each other."

"We're in a funny place right now. My fault. She's been nothing but loving and understanding as I muddle along figuring things out."

Fiona frowned, set her drink on a table, and crossed her arms over her chest. "Whatever are you talking about?"

He summarized the struggles he'd been having since leaving the priesthood and the guilt and uncertainty as he and Meryl grew closer. He ended by saying, "As I said—all me."

"Joseph O'Leary, that is the biggest load of horseshit I've ever heard. As you well know, I'm a good, loyal Catholic, but we're no longer in the Dark Ages. I do not believe in self-flagellation or guilt. You were a wonderful priest, and God knows what this family would have done without you all those years ago, but now it's time for *you* to live.

"You've found love and that's the most important thing in this world. Since you've been seeing Meryl, I've never seen you so happy. This is where you're meant to be, my darling son. Not weighted down by your robes and vestments. God wouldn't want that any more than your parishioners. We're thrilled and happy for you."

He smiled at her. "Some don't seem to want to let go."

Fiona waved her hand, shaking her head. "If you're talking about Martha Brewer, forget her. She's always had a crush on you, and look what the poor woman has to live with. That horrible bully."

"You know I can't comment."

"Well, I can. Now you listen to me. You've set up your practice, and the village is lucky to have you. I would suggest sending a letter to any of your clients who are members of St. Mary's to outline the parameters of your professional relationship. Tell them in a friendly but firm way that if they're not able to respect the boundaries, you can refer them to another therapist. Period, end of story."

"Uh-oh," Murph said, coming up behind them. "Sounds like my mother is giving advice and laying down the law."

Fiona turned and swatted her son's arm. "Hush, you!"

"Don't listen to her, Joe. She's never happier than when she's lecturing someone."

Joe grinned. "How's the groom tonight?"

"Excited, keyed up," Murph said, grinning from ear to ear.

"I'll leave you two to rehearse. I've got dinner to put on the table." As she passed Joe, she squeezed his shoulder. "You're a dear, lucky man, Joe. Don't you forget that."

"What was that about?" Murph said, looking up at him.

"My confused, mixed-up life."

"Love hurts sometimes till you figure it out. So glad Greta and I got through our stuff. You and Meryl will too. I hope it's soon. She's been moping around for a month. Thinks no one notices, but we all do."

"Do what?" Rori asked, joining them.

"Guy talk," Murph said. "Mom's gonna be ringing the dinner gong soon. Shall we?"

As they walked into the house to join the others, Rori whispered, "Teagan's one gorgeous guy. Where has he been all my life?"

Teagan Waite, the forty-three-year-old bass player for the Cherry Pickers, had stopped in for a drink to check last-minute details about the reception. They'd hired the band to play at Field and Fire. Blond with blue eyes, Teagan was a long-distance runner. His day job was as a biologist at the lab in town, where he worked with Richard's daughter Ava and her husband, Dan Fielding.

"Right under your nose," Murph said, exchanging a look with Joe. "You've seen the Cherry Pickers a bunch of times."

"But not up close."

The two men laughed. "Well, here's your chance, then."

"Ha-ha, your sister's already snagged him."

"Darby has a boyfriend."

"Well, where is he?"

"Back in Ohio. They couldn't leave the farm. Someone has to take care of all those goats, chickens, pigs, and other rescues."

"Exactly. While the cat's away, she does what she wants, and she wants Teagan bad."

"I wouldn't worry," Murph said. "She's leaving Sunday and he'll be all yours."

"Ha-ha."

In lieu of a rehearsal dinner, Greta and Murph wanted a simple family dinner. They considered Joe family, as well as Sandy, Pam, and Rori. Both of Murph's younger siblings, Darby and Seamus, were there, from Ohio and Hawaii respectively. Before they knew it, Fiona had invited Teagan to dine with them, an invitation he happily accepted.

Animated conversation and great food made for a lively dinner.

Joe, seated next to Greta, mostly listened, and enjoyed the family's banter. Her Aunt Sarah had spent the afternoon with them, but decided to remain at the cottage and relax for the evening. Her son Ralph, who had accompanied her from Carmel-by-the Sea in California, agreed to stay with her and look after Daisy, their pet goat.

"It's quite a group, isn't it?" Greta whispered to Joe.

"Yes, I'm sorry your aunt and cousin couldn't make it."

"Jet lag."

"You're marrying into a great family," he said.

"Don't I know it? As an only child, I think this is very precious."

"You are too," he said, smiling at her. "They are fortunate indeed."

"I could say the same to you. I'm so glad you and Meryl found each other. I've never seen two people so in love."

"Thank you," he said, turning to the others as Murphy Senior stood up to give a toast.

Do others see the truth and not me? he thought as the elder O'Neill turned to gaze at his son. A family that had suffered such a terrible loss with Aislan's death treasured every moment together and appeared to never take that for granted. How he loved and respected them.

Booked solid from four to ten, Field and Fire was hopping, and Meryl never stopped. Since the launch of the new menu, they'd been besieged by food critics and foodies from far and wide. Thus far reviews had been favorable, hence the increased interest. With Sandy, Rori, and Murph out, she worked the front and back in the kitchen. Lucy, Richard, and Callie had come to help out, and Wolfie manned the bar. Thankful for the distraction, Meryl threw herself into her work.

As the last guests said their good nights, workers gathered in the large dining room with a drink. "Thank you all!" Meryl said. "Couldn't have done it without everyone, including our visiting staff." She smiled as she gazed around at the Morgans, Callie and Wolfie.

"You've given a much-deserved night off to Murph, Sandy, and Rori, as you did for me recently, and I can tell you, it's an amazing gift. I love you all." Unexpected tears rimmed her eyes as Meryl sat down.

Everyone clapped. "Hooray for the boss!" Freddie cried, raising his beer.

Lucy rose and came to sit beside her. "Are you okay?"

"Yes, sorry for getting emotional. Just tired, I guess."

"Pam told me things have been up and down with Joe." Glimpsing Meryl's surprised expression, she added, "Sorry. Small town, big close families who tell each other everything. The good news—in my experience—everyone cares about each other's happiness."

"It's okay, thanks," Meryl said. "It's been a while since I've been in a relationship, and this one's been a roller coaster. I know he's going through a huge change, and I'm trying to be supportive. It's exhausting."

"I'm sorry. If there's anything we can do, please ask."

"Look what you did tonight. You were all so helpful, and Callie is amazing. Wish we had her full-time."

Lucy laughed. "My husband would collapse without Callie, and not just her cooking. But seriously, Meryl, I know you work most nights, but any time you're off and you'd like to come for supper, we're usually at the farm with one or more of our offspring, spouses, grandkids, whoever, and we'd love for you to join us. You don't even have to let us know. Just show up for drinks around six and off we'll go."

"I second that!" Richard said, coming to sit beside his wife, arm circling her shoulders.

"Thank you both," she said as people stood and prepared to leave.

"Any other chores before this old man heads home to bed?" he asked.

"No, we're good."

"You brought the flashlight, right?" Lucy said to him.

"Wolfie's got one."

"Much as he loves his dad, I don't think Wolfie will be strolling back with us," Lucy said as she gazed toward the kitchen door where his son and Lyddie were just disappearing. "It's a clear night and a full moon. We'll probably be fine."

"So glad they've made up," Richard said.

Meryl stood. "We have several flashlights in the kitchen you can borrow. I'll grab one."

After saying good night to her staff, Meryl headed to her car. Once inside, she rested her head against the steering wheel and let the tears fall. Sobs racked her body as she finally let go of the feelings she'd tamped down all day. Fortunately, she'd parked away from the building and her Mini Cooper was by itself, apart from the others' cars so no one noticed her alone and weeping.

When her tears dried, she took several deep breaths and started the car. Calmer and more peaceful, she turned down the long driveway. As she passed the winery, she spied Wolfie and Lyddie heading into the main building and smiled. As lights blinked on in the upstairs apartment, she thought, *maybe he's finally ready for the big move?*

Once out on the main road, she pushed the button on her phone and called Johnny.

"Hey, beautiful," he said after answering on the first ring.

"Hey."

"That doesn't sound like my optimistic, upbeat sister. What's wrong?"

"What do you think? It's Joe, always Joe." She gave him a quick recap of what had happened on their walk in Southport.

"A minor hiccup?"

"Doesn't seem like it. I think he believes we were a mistake, something he shouldn't have done. Guilt? Regret? Who knows?"

"Do you want me to hop on a plane?"

"We could have used you tonight with Sandy, Murph, and Rori off."

"What?"

She explained about the rehearsal dinner.

"Oh jeez, I forgot, tomorrow's the wedding, right? Are you going to be a guest?"

"Hardly. We've got the reception here, and the rest of the restaurant is booked solid."

"Good for you. I read two online reviews yesterday. Field and Fire's headed for stardom. Now seriously, I'm retired. I can come back and spend a few weeks providing moral support for my favorite sister and an extra set of hands at Field and Fire. I don't have to be in Saguaro Valley for another three weeks."

"You're sweet, but I'm okay. After tomorrow, I'm going to crash at my house. Grab a good book and lie on the sunporch watching the river."

"Sounds sublime."

"Someday, I want to come to Saguaro and see Emma's Dream," she said, the western Morgan's summer camp for handicapped children. "I can return the favor and help you out."

"Love it! I have a fun, laid-back staff, and my worker bees change every summer since counselors grow up and leave us."

As she pulled into her driveway, Meryl smiled. "Thanks, big brother. I needed to hear your voice."

"Well, you'll be hearing it more because I'm calling every day from now on."

"Not if you're busy."

"Retired, remember?"

"And volunteering every day of the week somewhere." Johnny cooked lunch and dinner five days a week for one of Chicago's largest Boys and Girls Clubs. He also made baked goods, which he delivered to a senior living center two blocks from his condominium.

"Only five days. And I meant what I said. I can grab a ticket and be there in three hours."

"If I get to the end of my rope, I'll send an SOS."

"Night, sweetie."

"Night."

She unlocked her front door and slipped inside. "A shower and bed," she said aloud to the empty house. "Maybe I should get a dog."

CHAPTER 30

While Quaker weddings typically had no officiant, Murph and Greta had broken with tradition and asked Joe to preside. They kept the custom of no one giving away the bride, and the couple walked in together, hand in hand after everyone was seated. Greta looked exquisite in a short lace trimmed dress with capped sleeves that hugged her slender frame and showcased her lovely legs. She wore flowers in her hair and carried a bouquet of white roses and baby's breath, intermingled with delicate greens. Tears in her eyes, Meryl watched from the back pew as the couple passed by. Her stocky Irish colleague, often described as built like a brick shithouse, looked handsome in his dark suit, his face reflecting peace and certainty as he shepherded his bride to the opposite side of the room where Joe stood.

The tall ex-priest looked gorgeous in his dark suit, white dress shirt, and tie, its colors like the ocean's blues and greens. He stood straight and impossibly tall as his warm smile greeted the bride and groom. Meryl's heart skipped a beat as she watched him and was startled when he looked up and met her eyes with the same warmth. Only for a second, he then turned his attention back to Murph and Greta.

"You look beautiful, my dear," he said, to Greta, "and your groom cleans up pretty well." His eyes lingered slightly longer on Murph, the strong young man he'd watched grapple back from tragedy's brink so many years ago. "Welcome all."

He then shared the familiar verses of Corinthians 13:4–7, which Murph and Greta had chosen. As he read, the words struck especially deeply as he thought of Meryl and their relationship. *Love is patient and is kind. Love doesn't envy. Love doesn't brag, is not proud, doesn't behave itself inappropriately, doesn't seek its own way, is not provoked, takes no account of evil; doesn't rejoice in unrighteousness, but rejoices with the truth; bears all things, believes all things, hopes all things, and endures all things.*

At the conclusion of the passage Joe had recited by heart, he looked out and found Meryl, their eyes meeting for a second. *Yes, my love,* he thought, *love doesn't seek its own way. What a fool I've been.* Rapt in each other, the bride and groom didn't notice his second of inattention. Both looked up with expectation as he invited them to say their vows.

After the vows, Darby rose and read Shakespeare's Sonnet 18, which Murph had chosen. *Shall I compare thee to a summer's day? Thou art more lovely and more temperate...*

After, they exchanged rings and signed their license, Belle Pollart, Clerk of the Meeting, stood. Another Darn Yarner, she had muscles of iron from years of manual labor running the docks and fish market in Horseshoe Crab Cove with her husband, Will. Her cropped salt-and-pepper hair framed a handsome, oval face, deep-chocolate skin offset by her tailored white suit. She smiled, her dark eyes twinkling as she scanned the room. "This is the point where we observe a period of silence, and then if anyone feels moved to speak, that would be welcome. I'd suggest fifteen minutes of silence respecting the sacredness of this time for Murphy and Greta before anyone speaks."

Several people rose to offer congratulations and well wishes. Then, the silence was broken forty-five minutes later as Seamus stood. A smaller version of Murph with broad shoulders, red hair, and rosy cheeks, his rich, deep voice sounded to the rafters as he read e. e. cummings's, "somewhere I have never traveled, gladly beyond."

After Seamus took his seat, Belle stood. "I believe Joe has one more duty."

A wide grin on his face, Joe rose and gazed down at the couple. "It's my honor and privilege to now pronounce you man and wife."

Usually calm and shy, Greta jumped into her husband's arms, and he lifted and twirled her as they kissed. The Meeting House erupted in applause as the couple made their way around the pews and into the sunshine beyond.

Belle and Joe stood side by side and she leaned to him. "I guess we can't remind everyone to exit in silence at this point, can we?"

"Another tradition broken?"

"But joyfully," she said, taking his arm as they made their way to the door.

"Thank you, Belle. It was an honor to stand beside you."

"My pleasure. I sensed an unsettled spirit in you, Joseph, especially evident as you read from the Corinthians. May you find joy and the love you deserve, as we all deserve. She just slipped out, I believe."

"Off to work. The restaurant spared her and her colleagues for the ceremony, but I'm guessing she had to run."

"Good luck to you, son," she said, placing both hands on his wrists. "You deserve every happiness."

"Thank you," he said as they parted, once again astounded at the rapidity with which news spread in their tiny community.

As she'd exited the Meeting House, the tears began, and Meryl said a silent prayer of thanks for her parking space right beside the building. Sandy and Pam had offered to pick her up. Now she was glad she'd elected to take her own car. *A chance to recover,* she mused. *It was a beautiful ceremony.*

I should have begged Johnny to come, Meryl thought as she hurried to the storeroom for supplies. Swallowed up by orchestrating both the wedding reception and a busy Saturday evening in the restaurant,

Meryl was in her element, dashing back and forth from kitchen to dining room and veranda. They'd hired extra staff for the night, mostly servers, and with Murph as the guest of honor, Rori managed both rooms.

As the sun began to set, the veranda twinkled with thousands of white lights. Long tables covered with colorful linens and vases of wildflowers held all manner of finger foods with many vegan offerings. Servers passed hot appetizers. The extraordinary multilevel charcuterie board, affectionately dubbed Murph's cheese tower, sat at one end of the porch, with the bar at the other. Guests could also visit the bar in the small south-facing dining room, where dancing and dessert would happen later on. The room's French doors lay open to the veranda and the glorious water view beyond. The Cherry Pickers were setting up at far end of the room.

As Meryl stood with Sandy, observing the band members and the first of the guests arriving, he turned to her. "By the way, forgot to mention that Joe agreed to bartend in here tonight. Ready or not, here we go."

CHAPTER 31

"So the youngins have made up?" Richard asked, winking at Joe as he, Lucy, Lolly, and Jack stood near the inside bar watching Lyddie go by with a platter of stuffed mushrooms, headed for the veranda.

"Looks like it," Lolly said. "We haven't seen as much of her lately. And...a gorgeous vintner we know even checked into the inn the other night. Jack wanted to comp him, but he wouldn't hear of it. I invited them to stay with us, but you know my husband," she said, arm circling Jack's waist. "Complete neatnik. I'm not implying that Wolfie's untidy, but living with Mr. OCD can be a challenge, especially for a slob like me."

Jack smiled and threw up his hands. "Don't get me started. I'm not obsessive, but I do like things in their place."

"I imagine our office is a bit uncomfortable for you with all the boxes and piles of books everywhere," Lucy said, referring to their mail order children's book business office in town.

Jack laughed. "You can't imagine how hard it was for me to step into Merlin's Closet when I first came to town. Only the depth of my feelings for your partner propelled me through that door."

"Nothing wrong with tidiness," Richard said. "I'm a fan of it myself."

Lucy smiled, exchanging looks with Joe, who stood listening quietly while filling the occasional drink order. "That is when you're not in the middle of one of your whirlwind projects. Then the house and office look like a tsunami's passing through."

"Ha-ha," he said. "Hey, Loll, your sister gets prettier each time I see her," Richard added as he gazed at the Cherry Pickers tuning their instruments. Marla, Lolly's pretty younger sister, was the band's petite green-eyed vocalist and rhythm guitarist, her long hair loose and flowing down her back. Her boyfriend, Richie Vivieros, played lead guitar and sang as well. Beside them were Teagan on bass and Ross "Sticks" Weinberg on drums. "Whaddya think, Joe? Is that the prettiest guitarist you've seen in a while?"

Joe smiled. "She's a looker. I see the family resemblance," he added, looking over at Lolly.

Lolly guffawed. "Yeah, right. If I lose sixty pounds and dye my hair blue and pink."

"Don't you dare!" Jack said, hugging her.

As he watched the couple's banter, Joe thought about how nice it would be to spend time with them with Meryl at his side. He'd seen her when he first arrived and Meryl had said hello, but after that, she was clearly busy with no time to stop and chat. He grinned, observing Rori talking with Teagan, who seemed interested, but also distracted by the demands of his fellow musicians. Finally, she let him go and hurried off toward the main dining room. Joe watched her retreat and soon saw reason for her hasty departure. Both Sandy and Meryl were watching from the main dining room door.

Greta and Murph circulated, greeting their guests. There was no receiving line, but they did manage to touch base with everyone. A large table for their family had been reserved inside the dining room, strategically placed so they could see the action inside and out through the walls of unobstructed glass and the open French doors. The O'Neills and Greta's Aunt Sarah were already seated with full plates. Another table had been set aside for the bride and groom, his siblings, and her cousin Ralph, as well as Sandy and Pam. The rest of the tables inside and out were open seating with plenty of floor space left for dancing.

"Hi, Joe," Greta said, reaching to squeeze his hand. "The ceremony was perfect. Thank you."

"Sure was, buddy," Murphy said. "I owe you big-time. How about a few months of free lodging?"

Joe smiled, nodding as someone approached for drinks. "Not necessary."

Greta gave him a warm smile. "Can I have one of the servers bring you a plate?"

"Thanks, but I'm fine, and you have other things to do." He turned away from the couple to greet Frankie and Helen Winthrop, Lucy's Mom. Right behind them came Kyle and Harriet, who veered off to hug the bride and groom.

Joe poured the white wines both Frankie and Helen had requested. "Here you are, ladies."

"Thank you, Joe," Helen said, standing tall and straight beside her dear friend. He didn't know either woman well, but he admired and liked them. They always appeared so calm and at peace with themselves and their surroundings. Perhaps it was their Quaker roots? Both were dressed in peasant dresses popular thirty years earlier, Helen's pale blue and Frankie's deep emerald green. He wondered if they'd shopped for them together long ago.

"It was a beautiful service," Frankie said. "Greta and Murph looked radiant."

Helen nodded. "Radiant and happy."

"Enjoy your evening," Joe said, as they stepped back to allow others to approach the bar. *And I will endeavor to enjoy mine, content with brief glimpses of her,* he mused as he spied Meryl crossing the room with a small tray of food.

As twilight gave way to darkness, the full moon shone its light across the river. Suddenly, a collective sigh went up as Fiona O'Neill's enormous wedding cake appeared. A work of art, its five tiers were festooned with flowers real and edible. Applause sounded throughout the room as two servers set it on the table.

"Your mom's amazing," Rori said to Murph as the room filled up with guests for the cutting of the cake, one tradition Greta and Murph had kept.

"Yeah, she is. Fruitcake isn't to everyone's liking, though, so I hope people eat some of it or she'll be bummed."

Greta turned to him. "Did we make a mistake asking for the other cookies and squares? Now I'm feeling bad. Even though I'm not crazy about fruitcake, I would never want to hurt her feelings. I mean, look at it!"

"No worries. We'll cut it, they'll slice and serve it, and people can take home the leftovers."

Greta stood on tiptoe and kissed him. "My practical, wonderful husband."

"Hey, just being a husband, and I love fruitcake. You know we're taking at least one layer home for the freezer," he said, then he kissed Greta's cheek and winked at Rori over her shoulder.

ALONGSIDE THE WEDDING CAKE, NOW HALF GONE, WERE PLATTERS OF beautiful cookies, lemon squares, and tiny vanilla and chocolate pots de crème. Coffee and tea stations were at either end of the long table as well as on the veranda bar. As people sat inside and out enjoying desserts, Murph signaled Marla, and the musicians took their place. As strains of Bon Jovi's "Always" began, he reached out his hand to Greta. The love shining in their eyes brought many in the room to tears. It was no secret that Bon Jovi was one of Murph's favorite bands, and Greta had graciously ceded the first dance selection to him.

Soon the dance floor filled with couples. Meryl stood watching in the doorway leading to the main dining room, then turned away. "Good job, boss," Rori said.

Meryl sighed. "Thanks."

"Looks like we're winding down out here," Rori said, waving at the main dining room where only two tables were still occupied, the diners clearly readying to leave. "What say we wrap this up and go back for a dance or two?"

Meryl smiled. "Pretty soon." She turned and headed for the kitchen. By the time she returned, the dance floor was writhing. She'd removed her apron, combed her hair, and applied a touch of lipstick, but she couldn't say why. Clearly, she wouldn't be dancing. She gazed over at the bar, where she spied Joe chatting with Lucy and Richard, who appeared to have just come from the floor. Her heart fluttered as she watched him, missed him, ached for him.

ACROSS THE ROOM, RICHARD SPIED HER GAZE AND TURNED TO JOE. "Hey, buddy, Lucy and I have been dancing for hours. I'll man the bar. You take a turn. She's at the door."

"I can't leave the bar."

"Yes, you can," Lucy said, joining her husband behind the counter. "Between the two of us, we can handle any order that comes our way. Go. We promise not to poison anyone."

"Well, okay, then," Joe said, smiling as he ran his fingers through his hair and stepped around the end of the bar, deciding how to negotiate a path to Meryl.

Meryl had watched Joe leave the bar, but her view of him was obscured by dancers. As she observed Richard and Lucy serving aperitifs, a voice from behind startled her. "May I have this dance?" Joe held out his hand.

"Oh...well...yes," she said, laying her hand in his as the music shifted to a slow dance.

"Well, would you look at that. We did good, huh?" Richard said, drawing Lucy close and kissing her temple as Marla stepped forward to sing Dolly Parton's "I Will Always Love You."

Lucy laughed. "What did you imagine was going to happen, you old romantic?"

"What can I say? I believe in love, and if that's not love, I don't know what is."

"You're right as always, my love," she said, turning to hug him. "And look at your youngest. Could he get any cozier with a certain waitress?"

"Cute. Where's Jack? He must be ready to run out with his ruler."

"After all their recent sleepovers, I think we're beyond the ruler stage. Now get that man a beer," she said, grinning at Will Pollart, Belle's husband, who now leaned against the bar.

"Dolly has a beautiful voice," Joe said as he pulled her closer.

"Yes, she does," Meryl replied, wondering if someone had suggested they play this song, namely Rori. Her head chef stood next to Teagan, a tambourine in her hand, which she didn't appear to be playing. As the evocative melody filled the room, Meryl gave herself over to the music, resting her head on his strong, warm chest.

"I've missed you so, my darling," he whispered, lips brushing her hair.

"And I you." She moved closer and pressed her body against him, his growing arousal tickling her belly. As if time had stopped, they moved in their tiny circle, lost in a world that only had each other.

As the song ended, Joe hoped his erection would escape notice in the crowded space. Fortunately, his slacks were loose. He gazed down at her. "Can we talk? I'm sure Richard and Lucy will spell me for a few more minutes. I mean, if you're free?"

"I'd like that."

CHAPTER 32

Holding hands, they slipped out the door to the main dining room and made their way across the darkened room to the restaurant's octagonal bar that overlooked the water. Meryl led the way, closing the door behind them. Seconds after the door clicked shut, they found each other. Hungrily, they kissed, tongues teasing, begging. Her arms around his shoulders, Meryl ran her fingers through his hair, and Joe pulled her closer, stroking her back, his right hand moving to her waist, then tentatively upward.

"Wait," he said, and abruptly stepped back, holding her at arm's length. "Believe me, I want you right now more than anything in the world. Every fiber of my being burns for you, but I think we should talk first."

"Okay."

"Can we sit?" he asked, his hands still gripping her shoulders.

"Of course." She gestured to a table by the window. The full moon's reflection on the water shone through the wall of windows shedding light as they crossed the room.

They sat opposite each other, and Joe reached across and took her hands. "I've been a stupid fool, Meryl. The stupidest. Can you ever forgive me?"

"There's nothing to forgive." Her smile softened in the moonlight.

"That's kind of you to say, but I disagree. This, you and I, this is why I left the priesthood. I wanted a life that I shared with a loving partner. I was blessed to find her right in front of me and what do I do? I run away to Maine instead of staying and working through things."

"This has been a huge life transition in a short period of time."

"No excuse. Everyone goes through transitions."

"Well, I forgive you," she said, squeezing his hands. "I'm also pretty sure we're going to be missed out there pretty soon."

"Yes. At least this chat has tamed my arousal enough that I can go out in public again."

She laughed. "Too bad. I was hoping for a quickie. Can I say that at age forty-two? A quickie?"

Joe chuckled. "This is why I love you so. Yes, you can say quickie to me, anytime you want. Of course, it sends my long-dormant libido through the roof, especially when we can't act on it."

Meryl stood, holding out her hand. "Well, I'll just have to make sure to say it next time we're in a position *to* act on it."

"I'll sure look forward to that." He circled his arm around her shoulders, drawing her nearer as they reached the door. "One kiss?"

"I was hoping you'd say that," she whispered as his lips captured hers in a searing kiss that left them both short of breath and wanting more.

As they reentered the small dining room, he said, "I'll call you tomorrow," and they separated, Joe to the bar, Meryl to supervise the servers who would be starting serious cleanup soon. He watched his love move about the room and marveled at her incandescent beauty, her kind gestures, and her competence as she interacted with her staff. Cold now without her beside him, he realized he hadn't truly felt warm since their walk in Southport. The walk when he'd stupidly pushed her away.

The band announced last song, and then it was time for Greta and Murph to depart. They were staying in Providence for the night before their flight to Bermuda. They'd chosen that island because they wanted warmth. Its short travel distance meant they could get there quickly, as they could only be away five days. Lyddie would be staying at their house to look after Daisy, their goat. As Joe observed Lyddie wrapped around her handsome vintner, he suspected that Daisy would be getting plenty of attention from two instead of one. *Lucky Daisy, all that love*, he mused, chuckling to himself. At that moment, Meryl walked by, giving him a beautiful, intimate smile and he glimpsed his own happiness reflected in her luminous blue eyes.

CHAPTER 33

Before leaving for church Sunday morning, Joe phoned Meryl.

"Morning," she said, her voice cheerful.

"How are you?"

"Exhausted."

"I figured as much. I know these are your days off, but I'm committed at the O'Neills today and have a pretty full day Monday. Could we meet Monday night?"

"Unfortunately, I can't. There's a private party at the restaurant."

"How about Tuesday lunch? One? I have about an hour and a half between clients."

"Perfect."

"Meet at the Café or...?"

"Cafe's great. See you then."

"Meryl, wait."

"Yes?"

"It was wonderful to see you last night."

"You too."

As he clicked off the phone, Joe smiled, whistling as he grabbed his keys and headed for the truck.

~

A DAY TO MYSELF, Meryl mused, as she cleaned up her breakfast things. *Almost as good as being wrapped in his arms.* While disappointed that she wouldn't see him today, life had been so crazy lately that a day on her sunporch with a good book sounded perfect. Not sure what to think of last night, she decided to take things one day at a time. *From the depths to the pinnacle,* she thought, heading upstairs to dress.

Last night's reception had been a resounding success. Several attendees had approached her or Sandy about booking similar events. Meryl credited it all to Cady's amazing food, but Sandy disagreed and credited her with the lion's share of their success. Their next order of business was to hire additional staff, both trained chefs and servers. They needed another swing chef and an assistant entremetier or vegetable chef to work with Cady. Prepping the mountains of vegetables needed each day in her recipes was more than their current staff could handle, and Meryl and Rori were often called from their jobs to assist. Not ideal.

"I won't dwell on that now," she said aloud as she grabbed her book and headed back downstairs. "Housecleaning can wait until tomorrow too," she announced to the empty house. It was a glorious warm day, and she was determined to enjoy every minute of it.

Before settling on the sunporch chaise, she strolled barefoot to the end of the dock and sat watching the boats go by, gulls and shore birds soaring and swooping in front of her. Cormorants stood on nearby rocks, wings outstretched, sunning themselves. She spread her arms out wide, imitating them, closing her eyes, face turned upward to the sun.

"Beautiful day, isn't it?" a voice called.

Startled, Meryl opened her eyes and spied Frankie sitting in a deck chair on a twelve-by-twelve float attached to the end of her dock, coffee mug in hand. The women were less than ten feet from each other as the float was tied to the left of Frankie's dock.

"Good morning! Beautiful day, yes." Meryl already loved Frankie. Intrigued by her tall, independent neighbor and all her many professions, she especially liked stories about her private investigating business. Dressed in overalls, her wild curly salt-and-pepper hair tied back in a bandana, she looked like she might be headed for a day in her stained glass studio situated in an old barn she owned near the docks. "Are you off to your studio today?" she asked.

"It's Sunday. I try not to work on Sundays except for fun. The Darn Yarners are meeting in a few hours for lunch, then a work detail to turn over and prep our garden beds in town."

"How fun. How many beds do you have?"

Frankie grinned. "Four. We'd liked to have gotten eight, one for each of us, but we didn't want to be piggish. We somehow manage to grow bushels of vegetables and fruits. And we keep one bed for flowers, my favorite."

"You're so lucky to have each other."

Her neighbor nodded. "That we are. None of us take that for granted."

"Some of you single, some married."

"Women friends are different from spouses."

"You're right... I mean, I assume that's true. I've never been married or lived anywhere long enough to make friends."

Frankie peeked over the rim of her coffee mug. "Seems like you have lots of potential buddies living here."

"Did you live here in the village when you were married?"

"Oh, goodness no. Leonard could never live anywhere but in the city." Frankie's former husband, the highly successful architect Leonard Paltz, lived in Boston, but traveled all around the country and world designing commercial spaces. "We came here once on vacation and he broke out in hives. Too much nature."

Meryl laughed. "I like to visit the city, but this feels more like home."

"Especially now that a certain handsome someone has returned?"

"Yes."

"Sorry, I won't tease except to say he's one of the good ones, my dear. I've known Joe for years, and he's a fine person."

"Yes, he is."

Meryl stood and stretched. "Have a great time gardening. Maybe if I get bored with my book, I'll head into town for a sandwich and stop by to cheer you on."

"We'd love it," Frankie said, waving. "And feel free to bring your trowel!"

CHAPTER 34

Tuesday, Joe closed his office door a little before one and walked out with his last morning client, Betty Halligan. "Thanks honey," the fifty-something widow said, grasping his arm.

"You have a good day, Betty," he said, gently removing her hand.

"You're a love." Joe stepped back, and she got the message. "Well, ta-ta, lovie!"

He shook his head as he waited for Betty to drive away, then began walking down Main Street to the Café. Meryl waited by the door and waved as he approached. "Another beautiful day," she said as they exchanged a brief hug.

"Not as beautiful as you," he whispered.

The Café was crowded, so after placing their orders and paying, they stepped back outside. Josie Connors, who owned the Café with her husband, Paul, promised to send one of the waitstaff out with their food when ready.

"So how are you?" she asked as they stood in the shade.

"Good." He gazed around to ensure they were alone, then added, "Still working on the boundaries issues with my former parishioners."

"I thought you were going to send out a letter about that?"

He leaned closer, smiling, making sure there was no one listening. "I did, but some people either don't read their mail or chose to ignore it. The client who just left insists on calling me Lovie."

Meryl chuckled. "Aw, that's sweet."

"I can assure you, it's not."

"So, what's the answer? Another letter?"

"No, I'll just keep reminding people when they come in. It's a process. Tell me about you. How are things with you?"

She spent a few minutes telling him the latest at Field and Fire news until they were interrupted by Milly and their food. Joe took the bag, thanked her, and they headed down the street.

Once settled on a bench in the garden, they people-watched for a while, enjoying their sandwiches. Meryl had ordered what she almost always ordered, a BLT wrap, and Joe, a Reuben. "I continue to be so amazed at this space," she said. "My neighbor, Frankie Brown, was telling me about the four beds she tends with her fellow Darn Yarners. What a group they are."

"Yes, extraordinary women. This incredible space has brought the community together in so many ways." Joe nodded as Kitty Bannister, the landscape designer who had worked with Pam to create the garden, strolled by. Kitty now served as curator of the space and had also overseen the expansion to twice its original footprint. While no one knew who paid Kitty's fees for this work, it was assumed that most of the financial backing came from Richard Morgan and Mavis LaSalle, whose property abutted the garden. Mavis had donated both plots of land and was rumored to be considering giving them more acreage.

"Aren't we lucky?"

"Yes," he said, his eyes warm as he gazed at her. Both had crumpled their sandwich wrappers and placed them in the bag. "Do you have time to come back to the office for tea?"

"I'd love that," she said, taking his hand.

THEY STEPPED INTO THE SMALL, LIGHT-FILLED SPACE, AND HE CLOSED the door softly. The air felt electric, sparks flying between them as Meryl went to gaze out the window. "Someone's been tending to the garden."

"Yes."

"You?"

He nodded. "Kitty Bannister's been assisting. The tenants in the building pooled our resources to pay her fees."

"It's beautiful, isn't it?"

"Yes, it is." Clearly, he was not referring to the garden as he crossed the small space and took her into his arms. "I've been waiting to do this for what seems like years. I'm constantly distracted. I feel guilty because half the time I'm not listening to my clients. My thoughts are all of you." He cupped her chin in his hand and leaned down to capture her beautiful mouth in a deep kiss, communicating the desperate longing he felt in every inch of his body and mind.

Meryl responded, opening herself to him, her breath coming in gasps. As they broke the kiss, she whispered, "I feel the same. I've been aching for you day and night. It's been pure torture."

"Well, we can't have that," he said as her lips trailed kisses down his neck. Joe's hands moved to her sides, then to her round, perfect breasts. He could feel her nipples reacting to his touch, like ripe hard berries under her thin T-shirt.

Meryl closed her eyes, arching her back, begging him to take her. He took hold of the hem of her shirt and whispered, "May I?" Meryl nodded, then reached back and unhooked her lacy white bra. He gazed down, drinking her in. "You are so beautiful, my darling."

She smiled and began unbuttoning his crisp blue shirt. "I'm yours, you know."

"Not very romantic. You should be lying on a bed of rose petals. Are you okay taking this further, again in my office?"

"What do you think?" she said as she stroked his growing arousal. "I don't need rose petals, but I do wonder if we need all these clothes." As she spoke, she unzipped his fly and released him, then let her jeans and panties fall to the floor.

He turned and grabbed his pants, extracting the shiny packet. "I brought it just in case."

"I'm glad," she said taking him in her hands, stroking, massaging.

His hands moved from her breasts, replaced by his tongue and mouth as he laved and teased, taking one, then the other into his mouth. "Oh, oh, oh," she whispered, arching her back, giving herself over to a haze of sensation. As her orgasm ripped through her, she felt his fingers move between her legs.

Voice husky, he nibbled her ear. "I'm still not sure what I'm doing, but someday I hope you can teach me."

"You're doing just fine. I want all of you, Joe. I need you. Inside me. Now."

Withdrawing his hand, he ripped open the packet and sheathed himself. Before she knew what was happening, he'd lifted her, wrapping her legs around his waist as he moved to the wall farthest from the door. When his back touched the hard surface, he moved slightly, and Meryl reached down and guided him into her warm wetness, taking him deeper and deeper until he filled her completely.

"I love you," he whispered, holding her, allowing her to lead, then matching her urgent movements. When they reached a blinding, thunderous crescendo, Meryl fell against him and Joe held on, never wanting to let her go.

"Oh, my goodness," she whispered. "That was... I felt... I don't know how to describe it."

"Me too, my sweet."

Meryl kissed his shoulder, then let out a sigh. "Much as I love this, we should get dressed and you should open the windows and get out that lemony spray of yours. If this is going to become a habit, you'd better invest in a gallon of that stuff."

Joe laughed, then groaned as he withdrew from her luscious, warm depths. After gathering their clothes, they dressed quickly, then straightened the room. Lemony scent surrounding them, he pulled her to sit on his lap on the love seat. "I should cancel my appointments for the rest of the day so we can do that again and maybe again."

She kissed him, her hand stroking his cheek. "I have to be at the restaurant in an hour."

"I want to say something," he said, eyes full of love as he looked into hers. "It would be more romantic somewhere else, but I can't wait another second. I don't expect you to respond, but I hope you'll understand when I say it."

She smiled, cupping his face in her hands. "You've already used a lot of words and still haven't said what you want to say."

"I love you, Meryl, more than life itself. I feel like my entire life has been lived with the promise of you. I can't imagine another day without you in it. I want to wake up with you in my arms and fall asleep the same way. So... I wanted to ask you if you would consider... I mean, might you consider making me the happiest man in the world and consenting to be my wife? I'm sorry I don't have a ring, but we can look together and you can choose what you like. I'm assuming you want to think about this, but—"

"Yes."

"I know this isn't the best venue. We should be at a romantic restaurant or a beautiful spot by the ocean."

"Yes."

"Are you agreeing with me? Shall I wait and find a better spot for this?"

"I'm saying yes, I'll marry you, Joe O'Leary. I don't care about rings, romantic restaurants, or ocean views. You could propose in the closet and my answer would still be yes. Yes, yes, yes!"

Stunned, he sat back. "You said yes?"

"I did. Are you thinking of taking it back?"

"Absolutely not. Never!" He drew her close for a gentle kiss. "I do have one more question, though. Was this what's known as a quickie?"

"A quickie that lasts for the rest of our lives," Meryl said, kissing him back.

$\sim$

READ ON FOR SAMPLE CHAPTERS OF *EMMA'S DREAM,* BOOK ONE IN THE Morgan's Run series, where the already hot Southwest sizzles!

EMMA'S DREAM

Chapter 1

"This is a huge mistake," Ben Morgan muttered, his chest tightening as he steered the Range Rover over the Arizona mountain pass. "Maybe the biggest one I've made in five years."

Then he remembered it wasn't his decision. Doctor's orders propelled him eastward, away from his gorgeous new home in Santa Barbara and a rapidly expanding business, which needed his attention twenty-four seven. The partners, his college roommates, and dear friends, had assured him they could manage without him for a while, but the guilt was eating at him already. His stomach growled, but there was no place to stop in the desert that surrounded him. He would have to eat in town.

As the jeep climbed the Saguaro Canyon Pass, he thought back to the previous Thursday. On the Coast Highway, headed home for a swim in the ocean after a long day at work, he was still reeling from his last encounter with Miranda, his girlfriend of two years. Their official split had been several months earlier, when he moved out of their condo and into his new home, but unfinished business, mostly financial, had necessitated one more meeting, over lunch. The parting hadn't been pleasant, but they still needed to work together.

Miranda's law firm handled all his company's legal work, and the partners wanted to keep her on.

As he exited the restaurant, the pain started. Chalking it up to indigestion, he'd hopped in the car and endeavored to ignore it. Halfway home, the pain now excruciating, he almost blacked out but was able to pull over and call 911. He told the operator he was having a heart attack.

Several hours and a battery of tests later, the cardiologist smiled as she leaned over his gurney. "Fascinating diagnosis, Mr. Morgan, but totally incorrect. You've had a panic attack. I'm not sure what's going on in your life right now, but whatever it is, you'd better see that it stops now."

"So, I'm crazy? Is that what you're saying?"

"No, what I'm saying is that something's going on that's triggering your physical symptoms. Are you under a lot of stress? Did anything unusual happen today?"

"Just work and the end of a romantic relationship."

She shook her head, regarding him as one might a two-year-old. "Two huge stressors. Do you have a cardiologist?"

"Why should I? I'm thirty-one, for Christ's sake."

"Right, okay. Well then, let's pretend I'm your cardiologist. As your doctor, I'm ordering you to take at least three to four months off work to decompress."

"Three to four months! Now you're the crazy one. I have a business to run and—"

"Which you won't be running for long if the stress and anxiety cause a massive heart attack. Either take time now to decompress, reevaluate, and learn ways to live your life differently, or we'll be spending a lot more time together. Do I make myself clear?"

Now, six days later, he was headed to his family's ranch in Arizona, Morgan's Run, and his enforced R & R. He laughed, wondering if returning home might actually increase his stress rather than the opposite. The Rover crested the peak, and he began his descent into the verdant valley that stretched out north and south as far as the eye could see. An orographic effect created this green, moist valley, surrounded by desert over the mountains to the east and west. In the gorgeous valley, a largely undiscovered town existed, an oasis for its roughly three thousand year-round residents and an equal number of snowbirds, tourists, and wealthy vacationers who found their way through the passes at various points in the year.

As Ben Junior made his way into town, he passed familiar sights, largely unchanged. Nothing changed much in Saguaro. The Town Garage had a fresh coat of white paint. "Whoop-de-doo," he said aloud, making a mental note to drop the Rover off for servicing soon.

As he turned right on Main and headed toward Gracie's Diner, a horn blared and the clunker in front of him screeched to a stop. Ben braked, but not in time to stop the Rover before it tapped the rear of the clunker. Ben swore under his breath and backed up, pulling over to park at the curb. As he did, the clunker's driver leaped from her car, screaming and waving her arms. He shook his head. Foolish woman had left her heap in the middle of the street. Tall and slender, she wore Jackie O. sunglasses, a baseball cap pulled low on her forehead, a faded cotton shirt over blue jeans, and cowboy boots, the uniform for nearly every female rancher in the valley.

"Geez, Toto," he muttered, patting the Rover's seat. "We're not in Kansas anymore."

As she approached the Rover, Ben noticed her jeans hugged every curve, full breasts not quite obscured by the baggy shirt. He couldn't see her face, but he had to admit the rest of the package was intriguing and also vaguely familiar. He approached as she bent to survey the clunker's bumper.

"What's the matter with you?" she screamed, walking in circles, arms still flailing. "Oh, my God, oh my God, what am I going to do?"

Ben stared at her back, astounded at what was clearly a huge overreaction. Her car was fine, hardly a scratch on it, although it would be hard to tell with all the other dings. Then, just as quickly as it started, the fire went out and she flopped down to sit on the curb, head between her legs, sobbing.

"Hey, hey, it's not that bad, is it? We hardly touched each other. No harm done." He sat beside her, wondering whether he should pat her on the shoulder. Immediately, she quieted and looked up at him.

"Oh, my God. This just gets better and better. It figures."

Ben Morgan, the one person she expected never to see again, was sitting beside her. Could things get any worse? She leaned forward, hiding her face, wondering whether he'd go away if she sat there long enough.

"Maggie? Is that little Maggie Williams? After five years, I'm in town less than a minute, and the first person I bump into is you."

Maggie groaned and buried her head deeper in her arms, praying this was all a bad dream. If she hadn't had to make a quick run to the bank, she'd be at work in the cool, dark stables. "Please just go. I'm fine."

She could feel his heat, his nearness rattling her to her core. A part of her longed to lean against him and draw comfort and strength from his warmth, but the wiser half screamed *danger*. She kept still, hoping he would disappear.

"You don't seem fine. Look, I'm sorry." Ben placed a hand on her shoulder. It sent shivers of warmth all the way to her toes. "And I'm not leaving until I'm sure you're okay."

Oh no, you don't. Maggie stood and shook herself, stepping away from his electric touch. She put on her sunglasses. Another second near him and she feared she might actually swoon. His soft chestnut eyes regarded her with obvious concern. Although he looked tired and thin, Ben Morgan was still drop-dead gorgeous, in faded jeans and sneakers, his broad shoulders straining the seams of a worn Stanford T-shirt.

"I'm fine, really. It's been a crazy day, and you caught me at a bad time. I'm sorry I overreacted."

Ben watched her, wondering why a fender kiss had caused, so much distress. "Can I give you a lift somewhere?"

"No, of course not! I mean, thanks, but I'm okay now. No worries about the car. No need to get police involved. Got to get back to work."

"Where's that?"

"Sorry, I'm really late. Good to see you again. Take care."

She hopped into her car and drove away before he could utter another word.

What the hell was that? Ben thought back to his one memorable night with Maggie Williams. They had both left Saguaro shortly after that night, but a part of him always wondered if there was something more to explore with his brother Kyle's beautiful classmate. While he'd pushed thoughts of her and their one night of passionate sex from his mind, as he watched her drive away, Ben realized that he'd spent five years comparing every woman he met to Maggie Williams. His stomach growled, and he shook his head. *Enough, time to eat!* He left the Rover and walked the three blocks to Gracie's.

Chapter 2

Noon rush over, Gracie's was empty except for one booth occupied by a family of four savoring the last spoonful of a Gracie Gila Monster. The diner's signature sundae was made with Gracie's secret chocolate sauce, vanilla ice cream, and hot toffee sauce, topped with whipped cream, then sprinkled liberally with crumbled peanut butter cups. Ben was tempted to forgo lunch and go for a Gila but decided on a portabella burger instead. With a nod to the family, he sidled up and took a stool at the counter.

A young freckle-faced redhead, ponytail wagging, bounced up, flashing him a smile that lit up the room. "Hi, sir. Can I take your order?"

"Hi, yourself. I don't know you. Are you new in town?"

She regarded him quizzically with lots of eyelash batting. "No, but you're. I'd remember you. Been here three years. I'm a student at U of A, but summers I come up to Saguaro instead of goin' home to Yuma. Too hot. My dad works down there. Just passing through?"

Ben gave her the hundred-watt smile that made most women swoon. She was no exception. "You could say that. Name's Ben."

"I'm Stacy. What can I get you, Ben?"

"Iced tea and a portabella burger, lettuce, tomato, and lots of Gracie's burger sauce."

"Comin' right up."

Ben watched her disappear into the kitchen, relieved that he hadn't yet met anyone he knew. He wanted to surprise his parents.

Well—he *had* met someone, he mused, remembering the curvaceous, lush-lipped Maggie Williams. It had been all he could do not to sweep her into his arms and kiss away those tears. Once again, he wondered at the subconscious torch he'd been carrying for her. And what was with her behavior? *Who falls apart and sobs uncontrollably over a bumper tap?*

Half an hour later, as he savored the last bite of his burger, Gracie emerged from the kitchen. "Still a vegetarian, I see. Crime in God's country."

Ben stood as she came around the counter to grab him in a bear hug. At six-four, he had her by a few inches, but Gracie was at least six feet herself, a towering figure in a grease-covered apron and frayed jeans, her wiry black hair streaked with gray, cut short, and sticking out at odd angles.

"How's my desert goddess? Have you missed me? You look younger than when I left."

"Tush." She waved her hand, clearly pleased by the compliment. "Always were the biggest liar from here to Albuquerque. Are you home to stay?"

"No, just a break from the rat race."

"Your folks must be thrilled. Can't believe they won't be angling for you to stay on, what with your dad slowing down and your brothers scattered hither and yon."

"Is Dad okay?"

Gracie gave him a measured look before answering. "Course he is. Strong as an ox, but he's not twenty-five anymore. Could use the help, I'm sure."

"Gracie, this is me. Has something happened to Dad?"

"He's fine, dearie. Had a minor dustup last year, but from your expression, I guess he didn't tell you about it. Not my place. Let him or your mom fill you in."

He stared at her for a moment or two, knowing he wouldn't get another word out of her. "If you could keep my arrival quiet till I see them, I'd be grateful, Gracie."

Ben went for his wallet, suddenly anxious to be home.

Gracie waved her hand. "Not on your life! Put that city money away and git up there and say howdy-do to your folks."

He leaned over and pecked her cheek. "Thanks, Gracie. Great to see you."

"Good to have you home where you belong," she said, gently nudging him toward the door. "Hope it's for good."

Chapter 3

Maggie drove through the main gate of Morgan's Run and pulled into her usual spot behind the stables. She killed the engine and drew out her cell phone. When her father answered, she breathed a sigh of relief.

"How's my angel?" she asked.

"Good as gold," he replied. "What's the matter, sweetie? You sound upset."

"Nothing, just wanted to check in on you and Emma."

"She's napping. Should I phone when she wakes, so you can say hello?"

"No, I'll see her in a few hours."

"Mags, what is it? What's happened?"

"Ben Morgan's back."

"Oh? Bump into each other, did you?"

"You could say that. We had a fender bender, right on Main Street."

"You okay?"

"Yes, just embarrassed. When it happened, I freaked out. Made a total fool of myself, crying and wailing over a minor bumper tap. Thank goodness no one else was around."

"Glad you're okay. You gonna tell him about Emma?"

A truck drove up beside her, and Maggie spied Jeb, her assistant.

"Dad, I gotta go. See you tonight."

"Take care, honey."

Maggie waved to her assistant. "Hey, Jeb. You ready to tackle Tabasco?"

She referred to a spirited mustang they were training, the size of a small draft horse. Soon, his rider, a Border Patrol agent, would join them to participate in the final weeks of training. Then horse and rider would return to Nogales as a team, ready to keep watch in the mountains along the border.

"Ready when you're. You okay, boss? You look a little green around the gills."

"Fine, just tired."

"How's my little cutie pie Emma doin'?"

"Full of it, curious, into everything, just like most four-year-olds. She keeps my dad busy."

"How's the therapy going?"

"Not much progress. She's just outgrown her third wheelchair."

"Wow, has it been that long since the accident?"

Maggie nodded. The sadness sometimes overwhelmed her, etching new lines across her brow and haunting her dreams. Afraid to be far from her phone, she watched the clock until it was time to head home. It wasn't that she disliked the work. Maggie loved training horses, assisting with the day-to-day running of Morgan Run's stables, but she worried constantly about Emma. Two years ago, the toddler had just learned to walk when their car had been broadsided by a drunk driver.

Hands on hips, she stared at Jeb, who seemed a million miles away. "Are you coming or not?"

"Sorry, boss!"

He fell in step beside her as they headed for Tabasco's stall.

Chapter 4

Ben eased the Rover through the front gates, turned away from the house, and headed for the lodge. At this time of day, he was pretty certain Ben Sr. would be in the lobby bar greeting guests, offering them a drink and a handshake. Ben Junior parked and hopped out of the Rover, pausing to gaze up at the massive log structure. Newly restored from a much smaller building, the renovated lodge had been designed by his brother Sam, an architect who lived and worked in Flagstaff. Its new wings spread in either direction as if the lodge were a colossal condor ready to take flight.

Ben sprang up the steps and passed through the massive twelve-foot doors that stood open to the afternoon breezes. He scanned the lobby until he caught sight of his dad. At six-foot-six, Ben Morgan was hard to miss. A thick shock of gray hair curled at his collar, and deep blue eyes sparkled with warmth as he chatted with a group of guests.

As Ben approached, the elder Morgan spied him and paused midsentence. "S'cuse me, folks," he said, nodding as he extracted himself. He closed the gap to his son, arms open. "Well, look who's home."

After a hearty bear hug, Ben Sr. patted his progeny. "What're you tryin' to do, give this old man a heart attack?"

"Hey, Dad."

"Has your mother seen you?"

"Not yet. Just got here. Wanted to see you first. See how things are."

"Great, couldn't be better. Especially now that you're home. How long you stayin'?"

"A month or two, maybe more. If it's okay?"

"Okay? You kidding? We'll take you as long as we can get you. Forever would be great."

"Thanks, Dad."

"Better get over to see your ma, or she'll have my hide. I'll finish up the meet-and-greet and be over shortly."

"You look good, Dad," Ben said, and he meant it. His father hadn't aged a bit, his long, lean body in terrific shape, as always.

Remembering Gracie's words, he hoped that whatever had befallen his beloved parent had been resolved.

"Pshaw. Go on, now, git. Be down in a few."

Ben started down the lane to the house but decided to take the long way around the stables. As he turned the corner, coming round the north side of the barn, there she was, standing beside the clunker, talking on her cell phone. She was bare headed now, her sunglasses perched atop her head, holding back her long, thick chestnut mane, loose and falling around her shoulders. She was smiling, in animated conversation, a musical laugh punctuating her words. She was gorgeous, the gangly teenager all grown up, transformed into a voluptuous woman. Ben thought about Miranda. Stylish and chic, but oh, so skinny, a toothpick compared to this full-bodied, luscious creature. *Totally different species.*

Suddenly, Maggie caught sight of him, and the smile vanished. Her loose, open stance closed up, and she turned away.

"Emma, honey, gotta go. See you soon, sweet pea."

Turning back, Maggie watched Ben step from the Rover and steeled herself for another encounter. The man was magnificent, no doubt about that. To her annoyance, her treacherous body began to tingle from head to toe.

"Mr. Morgan, we meet again."

"What brings you to the ranch?"

"I work here."

"Oh?" Despite her defiant stance, he noticed that her lip trembled. *Don't know how I can change the dynamic between us, but she's sure worth a try.*

"I train horses, run the pony camps and lessons, and help organize most of the pack trips. Harley leads them, of course, and I do the day-to-day stuff." *You're babbling, Maggie Williams. Stop talking!*

"What happened to Princeton?"

"Dropped out."

"Why?"

"Look, it's been a long day. I've got to get going."

"Do you live here? On the ranch?"

"No. Still live in town with my dad."

"How's he doing?"

Ben racked his brain to think of conversation topics that might keep her talking. Gazing into those deep azure eyes, he discovered a warmth and stillness he'd never experienced before. Had it been that way during the one night they'd spent together? He didn't remember those eyes, but he could still feel her soft skin, still smell her scent, a mix of citrus and jasmine.

"He's terrific. Same old, same old."

"Still wrangling and taking care of the valley livestock?"

"He retired a few years ago, but he keeps busy."

"Give him my best."

Gazing into his warm, dark eyes, Maggie felt herself going weak at the knees. And there was that treacherous tingle again. *Control yourself, woman.* "Will do. Gotta go."

"I'd love to see your dad," he called, but she was already gone. Ben watched her drive away and whistled softly. *They don't make women like Maggie Williams in California.* He'd forgotten what he'd been missing.

Get Emma's Dream!

ALSO BY M. LEE PRESCOTT

Contemporary Romance

Mystery

The Ricky Steele Mysteries

Prepped to Kill

Gadfly

Lost in Spindle City

Poof!

Lady Love: A Cautionary Tale

Also, featuring Ricky Steele:

Jigsaw

Roger and Bess Mysteries

A Friend of Silence

In the Name of Silence

The Silence of Memory

Silencing the Pen

Well-Loved Romances

Widow's Island

Hestor's Way

Morgan's Run Romances

Emma's Dream

Lang's Return

Jeb's Promise

Rose's Choice

Hope's Wonder

Ruthie's Love

Polly's Heart

Kyle's Journey

Gus' Home

A Valley Christmas

Aria's Song

Tom's Ride

Bella's Touch

Morgan's Fire Romances

Lucy's Hearth

Tim's Hands

Pam's Garden

Rich's Dilemma

Lolly's Wish

Greta's Goat

A Horseshoe Crab Cove Christmas

Joe's Calling

Young Adult Historical Romance

Song of the Spirit

A NOTE FROM THE AUTHOR

I'm thrilled to bring you *Joe's Calling*! I hope I have been respectful and sensitive in describing Joe's spiritual journey away from the priesthood to another kind of life. This marks the eighth *Morgan's Fire* book. A contemporary romance series, *Morgan's Fire*, follows a host of strong, resilient women—and men— as they live, fall in love and prosper in their New England coastal village.

Thank you so much for reading *Joe's Calling* and returning to this close-knit community with me. I love the village and all the colorful, vibrant characters who inhabit it. If you liked *Joe's Calling* and are willing to write an Amazon review, I would be very grateful. If you would like to sign up for future book releases, giveaways, and occasional notices about my books, please visit *http://www.mleeprescott.com/* and sign up for my newsletter, then follow me on BookBub. I promise I will not share your address, nor will I flood you with emails. Do visit my site to read more about my books and hear what's next.

Finally, this book has been revised, proofed, and edited many, many times, but my intrepid assistants and I are human, so if you spot a typo, please email me at *mleeprescott@gmail.com,* and I'll fix it. If you'd like to know more about my other books, please scroll ahead to the next section.

Warm wishes,

M. Lee

ABOUT THE AUTHOR

M. Lee Prescott is the author of dozens of works of fiction for adults, young adults, and children, among them *Prepped to Kill, Gadfly, Lost in Spindle City*, and *Poof!* (Ricky Steele Mysteries), *A Friend of Silence, In the Name of Silence*, and *The Silence of Memory* (Roger and Bess Mysteries), *Jigsaw*, and *Song of the Spirit*, and her contemporary romance series,

Morgan's Run. And now book eight of Morgan's Fire, *Joe's Calling*, where favorite series characters and new ones continue to live and work in the vibrant small village of Horseshoe Crab Cove. In addition to her fiction, her nonfiction books are published by Heinemann, and she has written numerous articles in the field of literacy education. Lee is a professor emeritus at a small New England liberal arts college, where she taught reading and writing pedagogy. Her research focuses on mindfulness and connections to literacy.

Lee has lived in southern California (love those Laguna nights!), Chapel Hill, North Carolina, and various spots in Massachusetts and Rhode Island. Currently, she resides in Massachusetts on a beautiful river, where she canoes, swims, and watches an incredible variety of wildlife pass by. She is the mother of two grown sons and spends lots of time with them, their beautiful wives, and her beloved grandchildren. When not writing, Lee's passions revolve around family, yoga (Kripalu is a second home), swimming, sharing mindfulness with children and adults, and walking.

Lee loves to hear from readers. Email her at *mleeprescott@gmail.com*, and visit her website to hear the latest and sign up for her newsletters!

Visit my author website and sign up for my newsletter at
http://www.mleeprescott.com.
Follow me on BookBub *https://www.bookbub.com/search/authors?
search=M.+Lee+Prescott!*